Praise for DON'T DIE

"I finished your book DON'T DIE, and I absolutely loved it! It was one of the most unique books that I've ever read …. The book really made me excited for the future and what's to come, thinking from zeroth principles."

— C. Hampsher

"I just finished your book a few minutes ago, and I am astonished at what you've put together. It's truly a masterpiece …. What you're doing for humanity will not go unnoticed."

— R. Ramchand

"First and foremost, I'd like to extend my gratitude for you to be on the mission of rethinking who we are …. You're almost like an Obi-Wan—the only hope."

— A. Davidenko

"My mind is full of all the adaptations and small wins that I can make to lean into Zeroism. What a gift to spend an afternoon immersed in the flow!"

— E. Hannan

Award-Winning Books by Bryan Johnson

Code 7: Cracking the Code for an Epic Life
(for ages 7-10)

"A suitable addition to any school library that is looking for short but fast-paced stories that reinforce pro-social behavior."
– School Library Journal

The Proto Project: A Sci-Fi Adventure of the Mind
(for ages 9-12)

"Johnson keeps the middle school laughs going in this action-packed, accessible look at the pros and cons of advancing AI and technology, a contemporary tale certain to intrigue and entertain young readers."
– Publishers Weekly

Forthcoming Books by Bryan Johnson

Blueprint Recipes for Life
A DON'T DIE Cookbook

We the People
A Novel

DON'T DIE

DON'T DIE

By Zero

Venice, CA

DON'T DIE

Library of Congress Control Number: 2023949490

E-book ISBN: 978-1-940556-15-4
Paperback ISBN: 978-1-940556-16-1
Hardcover ISBN: 978-1-940556-17-8

Published by Zero
protocol.bryanjohnson.com

*May we have the courage to believe
that now is the very beginning.*

Table of Contents

Introduction

In the beginning of one of my favorite novels, *Zen and the Art of Motorcycle Maintenance* by Robert Pirsig, the narrator and his friend are set up as direct contrasts. The friend has a new fancy motorcycle and does not care to learn how to repair it. The narrator has a vintage motorbike and finds joy and utility in the process of learning how to keep it in top shape to make it last as long as possible. Around my early thirties, my body and mind were beginning to feel ... *vintage*. There really is no kinder word. I needed repairs that I had never learned how to do.

Then things grew dire. *Everything* about me was at stake. My very life was at stake. Instead of giving in to my own demise, I decided to go toe-to-toe with the Fates. David vs. Goliath. Bryan Johnson vs. Time.

The war began a few years ago at the exact moment I took stock of my health and realized that a decade of chronic depression and poor cognitive control during childhood and early adulthood had yielded permanent effects on every measure of my health and well-being. Every single one of my cells was worn down. At first, most doctors told me that this breakdown was inevitable. *Age*, they said, with a shrug. *A one-way battle*, they said. *No turning back.*

My motorcycle was broken beyond repair. My body was broken beyond repair.

I wondered *why* that was the case. Is it a biological limit? A physical limit? A resource constraint limit? Why wasn't I told all this earlier in life when it would matter more? Why doesn't society mobilize gargantuan efforts to defend against the one enemy that comes for us and wins?

I began to unpack what I was learning: What assumptions were stacked together in these doctors' claims? Would each claim hold up to scrutiny? Would they always, despite the latest or looming medical advances? Could I somehow undo all those years I lost to depression? If not, *why not*?

The Mexican salamander, the axolotl, can regenerate. The tiny "immortal" jellyfish, *T. nutricula*, can regenerate. You can cut a worm into hundreds of pieces, and each will regenerate into a full worm. Greenland sharks have been discovered in the wild living for at least four hundred years. Technically, turtles *never stop growing*. Biology has proven time and time again that aging is a choice, not a fate.

Maybe, I thought, I could at least turn the hourglass of time on its side for a bit to recover the years stripped away from me? Is time's arrow really only one way?

That's when I picked up a laboratory notebook and looked at the best and latest gold-standard scientific data and all the body's repair manuals I could find. I consulted the world's top experts and went all in to push the limits of what modern science can do.

Of course, I'm still losing. We all are. But I have won some key battles in the last few years.

Today, I methodically track hundreds of biomarkers to measure all seventy organs, using my body as a vehicle for extreme health experimentation. The goal is to push the boundaries of current longevity science.

All this adventuring is not without risk. I've swallowed a miniature camera about the size of a baby carrot, which passed through my entire digestive system, taking more than thirty thousand pictures the whole way, before settling into ... well, you don't want to know. I have taken metformin, a drug given to patients with polycystic ovary syndrome, diabetic nephropathy, and gestational diabetes. Metformin is not your grandma's soup. I've also taken rapamycin, a drug given to suppress the immune system for people receiving organ transplants. Now, I am also technically a genetically enhanced human, having just received my first plasmid-mediated gene therapy.

Perhaps this adventure sounds like it might be fun?

I promise—it's not.

Not at first, but it is the ultimate game play.

What's less fun is the unthinkable return to my former self, to the version of me in my youth in a state of constant ignorance about how my body, like Pirsig's motorcycles, worked. I pity that version of Bryan, being tossed to and fro by whim and fancy and terrible cognitive choices. Change is hard; being miserable is harder.

3

The adventure is what I now call Blueprint. Blueprint follows data, not intuition. It is guided by science, not folk tales. If you peek behind the curtain on many of life's assumption stacks, we see that even the most basic questions are due for a modern, scientific reassessment. Consider even the simplest of medical queries such as, "How much water should one *really* drink in a day?" Folk wisdom says eight cups a day. But is that right for everyone? How much is too much? Or consider sleep. What is sleep good for, and how do I get more of it? When is the optimal time to eat for sleep? What does the heart need to pump optimally and possibly forever? Or other basic questions: Can you reverse gum and dental decay? What about germline cells? Do sperm and eggs really accumulate mutations over time?

The Blueprint team is made up of scientists, doctors, and researchers. All have an explorer's mindset. Had they been born in the 1800s, they would be tinkering with electricity or searching for gold in the California hills. If they had lived in the 1500s, they would have started the Renaissance. If they had existed during the Ice Age, they would be the ones crossing continents on land bridges, felling woolly mammoths with cunning stratagems and inventing languages. They are always moving toward something better.

Some people are born into this world and never once question their narrative. To them, the world is not a causal nest of discoverable principles—it just *is*. However, the mindset of an explorer is altogether different—a wondrous thing. It *wants*. It *craves*. It is never satisfied until it encounters something different and never before seen. Within the pages of this book, I hope you will join me as an explorer in discovering new frontiers of being human.

When I thought about how to write this book, I knew that it couldn't just be the diet and health side of Blueprint. It had to be a plan for the future of humanity. Blueprint is more than a health revolution. It is more than a science or data revolution. It is a revolution of thought. Of action. Of actions *not* taken. As grandiose as that sounds, I admit to being paralyzed by optionality. Should I, in these pages, call a kind of constitutional convention to rewrite the tenets of how a body is governed? Should it be a Big Think book with sweeping generalizations about the nature and sources of human society and conflict? Should it focus on the cognitive biases that riddle the human mind and hide like a time bomb in the psychology or self-help section? After all, people love that stuff, don't they?

Many voices in my head debated this question. The ambitious part of me wanted to make it something epic that might be read hundreds of years from now. The part of me who sees society as nested systems built atop systems in a constant feedback loop wanted to write a kind of coding manual on how to rewrite the operating system of our relationship to ourselves, AI, and to automation. My self-critical voice wondered why anybody who didn't know me would care to read any of that. The rural, peaceful side of me just wanted to relax and enjoy the finitude of life, surrounded by my loving and wonderful children.

With these conflicting voices swirling around in my head, I decided to do the most natural thing I could think of. I gave a voice to each of the voices, like a cast of characters in a play— *Scribe*, *Game Play*, *Model Builder*, *Self Critical*, *Dark Humor*, Seeks *Authority*, and some surprise guests along the way. They each play a role. A part. We contain multitudes, after all.

The journey has only just begun. Like all explorers who have come before me, I hope the pages of this book can provide a path forward for those who travel next. I encourage my readers to share their thoughts about *DON'T DIE* with me at dontdie@bryanjohnson.com.

While I may not be able to reply to everyone, I read every message I receive. Your thoughtful insights—and criticisms—are always valued.

This is not a journey into the unknown. This is a journey to prevent the unknown from being all that's left.

Thank you, reader, for joining me on this adventure.

Bryan Johnson
Sometime in the early twenty-first century

PART I: MORNING

"If you want to build a ship, don't drum up the men to gather wood, divide the work and give orders. Instead, teach them to yearn for the vast and endless sea."

—Antoine de Saint-Exupéry

"Men Wanted: For hazardous journey. Small wages, bitter cold, long months of complete darkness, constant danger, safe return doubtful. Honour and recognition in case of success."

—Ernest Shackleton

1: What Else Was Left to Do?

Growing up, I couldn't see what was left to explore. By 1977, Neil Armstrong had already walked on the Moon. Albert Einstein had already made time relative to an observer. Isaac Newton had described the laws of motion. Edmond Hillary had made it to the top of Everest, and James Madison had already written the operating system of democracy as we know it.

What else was left to do?

What I didn't realize then but do now is that humanity is at an unprecedented inflection point. With the increasing speeds of technological advance, dare we imagine 2,499 AD or even better, 10,354 AD? Eight thousand years from now. Wouldn't that be fun? What wonders about ourselves and the universe will we know then? From that vantage, is it possible that they will see today and say, "Wow, they didn't know anything!" Will people from then look back on us as we do upon cavemen? Is humanity in its infancy?

There is still plenty to do. The knee of the curve of progress. But unfortunately, it looks like we've torn our ACL by letting our tools destroy, consume, and shape us. The very nature of the future and our existence is in question. Coincidentally—luckily?—we are about to enter a technological age where we can reprogram all the basic building blocks of both our environments and ourselves.

But before I get into that, I should introduce myself.

I'm Scribe.

Hi.

I'm taking notes now because this is my last day on Earth, and hopefully these notes will be made into a future book, which you now perhaps hold. Since I won't be here in ten years' time to write one of those prefaces we see for many books, I want to do something a little different: to say *right now* what I expect to happen in the ten years after publication of this book.

Hopefully, *DON'T DIE* changed things. Otherwise, why even bother writing it?

Here is my hope for this book, as clearly as I can state it: I hope that these notes have been taken up as an actionable plan for humanity to brave its unknown and precarious future and they become an archive and explanation for the origin of the ideas that save the world.

I've been consumed every day for the last many years with the question of what our conscious existence will be like at different timescales into the future. Can I contemplate what my children or their children's children will see? In one thousand years, where will our minds be? What will they concern themselves with? What about in ten thousand years? *One million years*? Can you even imagine? What if we are merely at the fetal stage of humanity's long and windy course through the known universe? What if we're still just single cells on a great road map of human progress?

If so, then these centuries we know now and think are so, so important are but our mere infancy. We needed to invent the printing press, electricity, GPS, Internet, AI, and all else, just to break out of this infancy.

As I write this, in the first quarter of the twenty-first century, the trend lines are clear. We are about to experience an evolutionary transition on a scale rarely seen, a transition whose closest approximation is the changes written by evolution from early hominids two million years ago all the way to humanity today.

And just like the details of that last leap, this next evolutionary chapter will be sufficiently large that all of Earth's best minds—that's us, humanity—don't yet have words or concepts to explain it. It simply sits beyond our imagination. It would be like explaining microwaves to a hominid stuck with a hand ax.

And as much as I dislike being born at an arbitrary time and an arbitrary date in the second half of the twentieth century, I am beyond excited for what comes next even if I don't see it.

On a societal and evolutionary scale, we have just begun the Age of Self-Directed Evolution. We are increasingly able to improve our biological and cognitive abilities by programming our genes, bodies, and software. Despite how advanced we may think we are in today's world, we are in fact stuck in the Paleolithic Age of our cognitive evolution. Given our relatively caveman-like state, might future generations look back on us and wonder how we did so much with so little?

The endpoints and goals for this journey are not as easy to imagine as it is to imagine taking a first step on the Moon, Mars, or the South Pole. It's easy to imagine walking because we've all done it. The imagination exercise is just replacing the background with a background image of Mars, and voilà, suddenly we can dream again. But other goals, harder goals, such as the next version of being human, cannot be easily visualized because we, by definition, *can't imagine them.* And because we can't easily envision it, this means that it is hard to mobilize attention, awareness, and motivation. We can't JFK it with a moonshot; we can't Babe Ruth it by calling out the home run over the left field fence.

We must use the brains that nature gave us, inefficiencies and all. Bodies, too. I heard recently that an ancient genetic variant likely helped people retain heat and prevent frostbite by reducing their physical size. A genetic variant that was adaptable for the Ice Age but is unfortunately still around and contributing to an uptick in modern arthritis. It is almost certain that similar genes and traits exist that control our cognition— adapted for hundreds of thousands of years ago but not for today.

We should be immensely grateful to our evolutionary past, but we must also recognize that we are tethered to it. At least for now. How do we move into the next stage of our evolution? How do we escape the cognitive Paleolithic?

I believe the great explorers of our age and tomorrow's age will succeed when they close their eyes and set sail *inward*. Will our brains be utilized for rational thought and knowledge mastery in the future or something entirely foreign to us today? We have Moore's law for computers, yielding staggering gains in computational power and speed. What laws and consequences will emerge for radical human improvement? Can we even identify them now?

Occasionally, I ask myself what I would do if I knew I was dying. The answer is what I have planned for today. The answer is that I would convene those who know me best and try to do something *epic*.

These notes will be a record of my final day on this Earth when I convened those closest to me and asked them to finally formalize a plan. A real plan. Not just weekend plans. I'm talking about *the Plan* for the future of the human species. I strongly believe that we need a major cognitive revolution if we are to solve the global challenges we face in our immediate and long-term future. Our species evolved before, and we can do it again, but we can't wait a million years. We must accelerate evolution.

What I'm saying is very hard to understand and imagine because it's in the dark. Can't imagine it yet, remember? But bear with me. We haven't evolved to deal with cooperating on a global scale, battling invisible gases and nonlinear chemistry that warms our planet, or retraining our brains every few years as AI takes over more of our work. How can we augment our own minds to allow us to take on these challenges? If we actually had the technology to reimagine how our brains work, over time, I bet that we'd get really good at it and be surprised with all the new things we can do and come up with. To be clear, this is not just getting "smarter" by today's outdated standards or increases in the confusing, multidimensional, and flawed concepts such as "intelligence." This is about using our brains in entirely new ways.

Ultimately, for our own survival, we are in a race against time. We need to identify the problems that pose the greatest risks and respond fast enough so that we avoid a zombie apocalypse situation.

The most important tool at our disposal is adaptability. We need to be able to adapt as fast as change.

I am right now in my house in Venice, California, waiting for everyone to arrive. This is most of the group I climbed Mt. Kilimanjaro with, some of my closest friends. Everybody said yes to the invite. I'm delighted. On the mountain, we persisted together despite some of the hardest struggles of our lives along the way.

The plan, if all goes well today, is to write and finish the Plan. We have to. And soon. Too much is at stake. Unfortunately, like the year I was born, I also can't choose when I will die. But I know it will be soon. Very soon. Tomorrow, in fact.

Ring.

Ring.

Oh, good. I think someone's early.

2: The Gang Gathers

Q: Who are we when no one is looking?
Q: Who cares?

Someone was indeed at the door.

Farm Boy: "Sorry I'm so early. I've been up since dawn."

All I could do was smile. I already knew Farm Boy would be early. As predictable as the sun rising. Farm Boy is *always* early. Some people can't help it. It's not their fault. They just don't have much else going on.

"I bet you thought you'd be the first to arrive," I said. "Not true! Model Builder beat you by a day. He wanted the best room. It's like he thought it all through already."

Farm Boy: "Oh. I don't mind where I sleep. I can sleep anywhere."

"That's actually really useful," I said. "Thank you. You know the gang. Blueprint with his portable cooling pad. Cognitive Bias with his CPAP. Bunch of princesses with their peas, if you ask me. There's an air mattress in the basement, actually. Are you good with that?"

Farm Boy: "Yeah, sure. Whatever."

"Oh, thank you. Thank you. That makes my life so much easier."

"Will I get to see the sun rise? Usually that's what gets me up. Or the crowing."

"No, I don't think so. There are no actual windows down there. But there's good air. And a nice painting of a few birds, I think."

"Okay, sure. That's fine."

"Model Builder is out back. He's never been to Los Angeles. He's reading a book on the history of water rights and aquifers from the Colorado River, I think. He's confused how this city even exists."

Farm Boy: "It exists because people wanted it, right?"

He always said what you already knew but had forgotten. I loved him for it. We all did. I hadn't seen him in years and forgot he didn't always have a piece of alfalfa sticking out of his mouth at all times, like Huck Finn.

"Right, right," I said. "There are some things he'll never quite understand. People are irrational. He never quite understood that, did he?"

Ring. Ring.

It was Self Critical and Game Play, arriving together, but only one new car in the driveway. They must have carpooled. Strange. As far as I knew, they haven't even spoken since

Kilimanjaro. Few of us had. I took a deep breath before opening the door. I already half knew what Self Critical was going to say.

Self Critical: "A *gravel* driveway? What is this, the Great Depression?"

I ignored him and hugged Game Play first, with a grand, genuine smile on my face.

I said, "Good to see you both. Really. Truly. I'm glad you could make it." I couldn't not welcome Self Critical in. He and I go back to childhood. "Even you, buddy. Good to see you, too." I hugged him hard. As hard as I could.

Game Play: "So what's the plan for this weekend?"

He always got straight to the point.

"In due time. In due time," I said. "First, just get settled. Model Builder and Farm Boy are already here. You should go fight over rooms first. Can I get you both a drink? The Algonquin Table was all about their martini brunches and look what they did—start all of modern New York publishing."

Game Play: "I'm good. I already had my four ounces of ethanol for the week."

Self Critical: "I'll take your nicest gin mixed with your cheapest tonic."

Ring. Ring.

It was Blueprint. He was the only one not on the group chat. The only one I invited individually because he wasn't even with us on Kilimanjaro. He had no idea what we went through. Of all the configurations I played through in my mind, I was most worried about how Blueprint would fit in the group, if at all. He was the stranger, the new one. But he's also who I spent most of my time with these days—my new best friend of the past few years, if 45-year-old men can have best friends, that is. More than half the group hadn't even met him.

"Blueprint," I said. "Thank you. It's really important to me that you're here."

Blueprint, with a warm smile: "Of course, Scribe. Do you mind if I put this IV bag in your fridge? In a couple hours I have to do a small transfusion."

"Uh, yeah," I said. "Of course. Use whatever space you find."

Blueprint: "And I have a few packages arriving throughout the day, if you don't mind. A pillow, sound machine, butterfly needles, and an air purifier. Just a small one. You can keep 'em when I'm done. My gift to you."

I nodded, as if what he said was totally normal. As if I'd even be around to use any of that.

"Of course," I said. "Your room is upstairs, to the right. The quietest one, with the best AC."

Self Critical came to the entryway with a gin & tonic he had already made for himself. I saw a few drops spill over the rim and fall to the floor but chose not to say anything. Was he *already* drunk? It's 11 a.m.

Self Critical, staring at Blueprint up and down: "Who's the vampire? Should I get a wooden stake? Some silver bullets?"

I turned to Blueprint to apologize, but he had already spoken up without missing a beat. Blueprint: "The sun is a silent killer." He looked down at Self Critical's swirling cocktail. "Even worse than ethanol, which is a, how shall we say, *noisy* killer."

Self Critical, walking away: "Oh, this should be fun."

"Ignore him," I said to Blueprint. "He's a sweetheart when things get real."

Blueprint: "Things are getting realer and realer every day. It's just about the scale you choose. And the time horizons for—"

"Sure, sure," I said, interrupting him. I knew where this was going. "I know. You're right. Let's get you upstairs."

Ring. Ring.

If I had to guess, it was probably Cognitive Bias at the door.

Wrong.

It was Seeks Authority and Self Harm. I swear, they are *always* together. They are bound at the hip. They both live in New York in their own cloistered world, and I even suspect they both have the group chat muted. I had to send an *actual letter* just to get a response from Self Harm. Seeks Authority literally never even RSVP'd. If I didn't need them so much, I'd be mad.

Self Harm was the first to speak: "Hey, man, how are you, Scribe?"

"I'm—"

"Me too, man. We had quite the flight. Red eye. I stayed up the whole time, playing poker online. I won the cost of the flight back though. Any chance I could get a coffee?"

"Yeah, of course," I said. "There's an espresso machine in the kitchen. Can I make you one?"

Self Harm: "Oh, I'd *love* that. A double, please, if you have it."

"Two?" I asked, with a gentle hug in Seeks Authority's direction. Seeks Authority and I had the weakest friendship of all the dyads in the group. We went to the same elementary and middle school but had fallen out of favor as adults. We seemed to grow apart. The biggest bond in our lives was what had happened on Kilimanjaro. We didn't talk about it much, but we just *knew* that after that trip, nothing would ever be the same. We treated each other like vets from the same combat troop. We had both seen war. We knew its horrors.

Seeks Authority: "No, I'm good. Unless you're having one?"

"Actually, I could use one too," I said.

"In that case, sure, if you're making it. I'd actually love one. I could barely sleep on the flight. Thank you."

Ring. Ring.

Cognitive Bias was at the door. He didn't look well. He had gained a lot of weight, and he was definitely yo-yoing up. Without saying a word, he nodded and walked past me. Typical.

Ring. Ring.

Of course, Relentless and Dark Humor showed up together, last and late. Relentless walked straight past me to the bathroom, bursting through the door like a marathoner and surely rehearsing in his head a story about what he had *already* accomplished by 11 a.m. on a Saturday.

Dark Humor: "I'm only here because I presume you're dying. Right?"

Great.

Everyone had arrived.

Now for the fun part.

3: Last Chance Saloon

Dark Humor was still at the door, waiting for me to say he was right. He was. I *am* dying. But even though I knew he knew and he knew I knew, there was an unspoken peace treaty to not mention it, forged in a quick moment of silence.

"Well," I said. "Depending on the timescale, aren't we all?"

Dark Humor: "Your historical tricks won't work on me, Scribe."

I said nothing.

Dark Humor: "Shame."

I almost got the impression he meant it.

Blueprint was walking around the house with a UV monitor. Which to the untrained eye makes him look like a Chernobyl nuclear technician or one of those people who take metal detectors to the beach as a hobby. You could hear him mumble numbers under his breath close to windows: "Three-point-five! Four! What are they thinking?"

Dark Humor found Blueprint by a window: "Hi. Nice to meet you, Blueprint. Is it true that if I shake your hand, I will be banned from all future Olympic events or ever holding a government job? I've heard the rumors. You have enough creatine flowing in those veins you could supply Gold's Gym for a week."

Blueprint, without lifting his eyes from the UV counter: "Creatine? What is this, 2002? Did you hear that from a weblog? A chat room? Don't be silly ... hmm, no, this curtain won't do at all ... besides, don't look at me. The IOC is one of the best sources of performance-enhancing drugs on the planet. Just look at their list. Those are the ones you know *actually work*. Beta blockers banned for shooting events. Trimetazidine for anything of any duration. Who needs to pay doctors when you can just check the annual banned substances list?"

Blueprint turned to me: "Scribe, I appreciate you hosting us and your hospitality, but these curtains do nothing for UV protection." He waved his hand in all directions at once, which I interpreted as a kind of universal dismissal of every choice I had ever made in my entire life. "The UV index on *either side* of these walls is four. Which means being inside is no different than being outside. But we're not outside. We're supposed to be inside, but this is no different than being outside."

Model Builder: "No, we're definitely inside. By every measure that counts. UV is not one of the relevant measures. 'Inside' gives shelter, protection, privacy, and legal status. It filters air and protects from heat. Inside is very different from outside. We are in fact *inside*."

Blueprint: "Hmm."

I wasn't sure how well Blueprint would fit in with the group. Not a good start. I sent a group text to try to change up the narrative:

We're all here. Everyone, please gather in the dining room downstairs at 11:00 a.m. I have an announcement.

I made a pot of coffee, which I knew all but Blueprint would appreciate. (He had already had his 60 mg caffeine ration for the day.) Outside of Blueprint, who was just meeting people today for the first time, the rest of us hadn't all been in the same room like this since Kilimanjaro. There were occasional group texts or meetups between a few of us, but mostly the group had fractured into their own respective worlds. Life in one's thirties and forties just gets in the way. It's way too hard to align the group's varied interests. And once we had all been cleared of any wrongdoing by the Tanzanian and American authorities, we didn't much want to talk about it anymore, either.

I found Game Play outside. Of all the members of the group, I missed him the most. His silence the past few years was really hard. I tried reaching out many times, but he seemed to have lost his way after Kilimanjaro. Unemployed for years. No romantic relationship for more than a few weeks. It's like nothing gave him joy anymore. Ever since I met him, he was searching for the next thing, but it's almost as if he had given up.

He was on the back porch in a rocking chair trying to throw pennies from a change jar into a mug across the porch. Didn't look to have made a single one yet. Dozens of pennies lay strewn about on the porch and even further, into the grass. Some are quite far away. He must not be concentrating.

"GP," I said. "I missed you."

I handed him a cup of fresh coffee and sat next to him. I picked up a penny and tossed it. *Clink*. Made it first try.

"Ha!" I said.

Game Play: "But that's not the goal. Getting it in the mug is trivial. The goal is to get a penny to come to rest on the flat surface of the table the mug sits on. It's much too far to put any spin or to throw it softly onto the table. The penny just rolls right off. So I *think* the only option is to throw it so precisely that the penny rolls or bounces into the mug but then *rolls out*, softly. And then the penny can rest on the table finally."

I tossed another penny. The very knowledge of the increased difficulty of the task made me overthink it. I missed the table and mug entirely. There was probably a lesson there. I thought about writing it down, but instead, I watched him throw a few. He seemed to be spinning the penny so that it stayed vertical in the air. If the penny made it just perfectly and hit the side of the mug just right, it would roll out, like a snowboarder dropping into a halfpipe and getting shot out the other side.

I tossed again. Hit the side of the mug, and it bounced back violently and off the table.

I asked, "Why not just try to get as many pennies as you can into the mug. You know, like a normal person? And just be happy with that?"

Game Play: "There are hundreds of thousands of people with better hand-eye coordination than I for that task. They grew up playing basketball or tennis or golf and know exactly how the feedback mechanism works between their perception, their mistakes, and the minute muscular movements of their hands and fingers. If I wanted to be the best, well, I would have to go back in time and start training in the womb of my great-great grandparents. But nobody in the world will be as good as me at getting a penny on *that* table, from *this* seat, if only I can figure it out."

Of all in the group who were religious as youths, Game Play had lasted the longest in Mormonism. He didn't announce that he was leaving the church until he was almost 40. He misses it the most of all of us, I suspect, despite adamantly being the one to claim the loudest that he wishes he had left the church much sooner. But his intensity there seems to be proportional to the depth of its claws into his psychology. I recognize the feeling. Life, work, and love—all of it—was so much easier when you got longevity points and there were a finite number of seats to work for and the strictures were clear about what is and isn't allowed.

Imagine going from a board game, where the rules are clear and comprehensible and the reward and success conditions are laid out, to the actual, real-world, clusterfuck of life, which has no meaning, purpose, or goals other than those we give it. Having to shake off the gameplay parts of a belief system was like throwing a member of an uncontacted tribe in the Amazon into the heart of London. It's chaos. It's indiscernible. I remember reading once that Bobby Fischer was so good at chess perhaps precisely because of his tendency for paranoid schizophrenia. On the chess board, it was useful. But in the real world? Not so much. Game Play had let his beard grow. He looked a bit like Bobby Fischer, come to think of it.

Part of me would sacrifice my entire writing career—I'd never write another word, I promise—if only Game Play would write down his observations on the kinds of games people play. He's by far the best writer of the group. I just write because it's the only historical currency I know, and my thoughts are mostly in words. But Game Play won't do anything unless he's the best in the world at it, and he's too afraid of not being the best at writing, if I had to guess. He takes on new tasks like a modern machine learning algorithm might if given the choice. Sparse rewards do nothing for him. He needs *reward* rewards. Like throwing pennies into mugs to roll out and bounce off tables. You either do it right or you don't, and the feedback is near instant. Unlike writing. Unlike religion. Unlike life. There is no "close." No "try."

"What are you working on these days?" I asked.

Game Play: "You're looking at it."

"Come on, I know that brain of yours. Something must be brewing."

Game Play: "I'm thinking that maybe if I bounce the penny off the porch roof, or maybe one of those wooden beams above and behind it … see what I mean? … Then maybe it would slow the penny down enough that it might drop down onto the table? But even then, it's got too much velocity and would probably roll or bounce out."

Perhaps the universe was deterministic after all. Game Play had wound up his arm and threw a penny so it bounced off the wooden beam and proceeded to fall way too fast to the table and bounce off, just as he had predicted.

I decided to get right to the point: "Come on, you must be doing *something* with those millions of dollars, right?" Fresh off leaving the Mormon church, Game Play and Devil May Care had sold a tech company they cofounded for half a billion dollars. Sure, he was officially out of both the rat race and the fealty race. There must be a next thing. Or was he struggling to find the next game?

"Let me guess ... you don't know what is left to compete at," I said.

Game Play: "That sounds so 'Woe is me,' but honestly, yeah, that's pretty much it.

"Some days I miss the longevity points, too."

Game Play: "To be told one's entire childhood that life is eternal, but you have to earn points, if only you do *this* and *that* in the right order. And then told *don't do this* and *don't do that* or you'll lose points and then to have that all stripped from you one day is ... tough. Very tough. And then all those arcade ticket longevity points you earned for the afterlife, to trade in for eternity with your loved ones? Poof. Gone. It can mess with any mind."

"I know, I know," I said.

"I have kids now; did you know that?"

"I did. A few boys and a girl, right?"

"Yeah. Don't get me wrong. They are the reason to keep going. They are the new game. They are everything I was ever promised and more. But there's just something … still … missing …"

I tried Game Play's throwing strategy by spinning the penny upright and putting backspin on it overhand, like I was throwing a lure from a dock. *Clink.* Made it into the cup! But I heard the penny bounce around and stay there.

Odd. I felt disappointed.

"You know, it's funny," I said. "I was so proud of myself when I first got the penny in. And now here I did it again. Same act. Same difficulty. But just your reframing of the problem and the solution makes it so I'm disappointed to *just* get the penny in the cup. It's almost worse. I got closer to the real solution but didn't get there."

Game Play: "Welcome to my life."

I noticed he hadn't had a sip of coffee.

I said, "Oh, come now. Drink your coffee, and let's think through a bigger problem. Besides, from here it looks like the table is sloped downward and outward. It's not flat. I think it's actually impossible."

Game Play took the coffee but was not swayed by my argument.

Game Play: "Do you know about finite and infinite games? James P. Carse? Finite games are those you play to win. Sports. Politics. War. Classical board games. Infinite games you play just to keep playing. According to Carse, there is only one game. Life. I think you're misunderstanding the reason I'm trying to throw pennies into this mug here, Scribe. You think of it as a finite game, don't you?"

"Yeah, of course. If it lands on the table, we win."

Game Play: "No. I don't think it's possible. Like you said ... the table slopes. We are too far away. The purpose is to keep playing. The purpose is that every time we fail, we still have something to do next. To try again. It's an infinite game. Carse was wrong. There are at least two infinite games."

I responded, "A difficult finite game does not automatically turn into an infinite game, does it? I can imagine a scenario where it lands on the table by accident or chance. Perhaps if you threw it as hard as you could at the mug which perfectly knocks it over, canceling all the force of the thrown penny, causing it to drop like a spent bullet. It's not infinite. That's being too dramatic."

For the first time since I sat down, Game Play looked straight at me. He picked up a penny, sprang his arm back like a baseball pitcher, and threw the penny as hard as he could. It hit right at the mug's lip, and the whole mug awkwardly spun once and fell over onto its side, spilling pennies off the table.

One of them, however, stayed at rest on the table.

Game Play stood up: "Thanks. I think that was your penny."

"I think so too."

"You win!"

"I thought it was infinite!"

"No, no. I just said that to get you to think outside the box. It's obviously a finite game. We play until one of us wins. But sometimes it's easier to shake belief systems than it is to shake the rules."

I couldn't help myself. I had to tell him. Life is not an infinite game, but if anybody was going to convert it into one, it would be Game Play.

"What would you do if you were dying? What game would you play?"

Game Play: "I am dying. We all are, right?"

"I know, I know. I mean, dying soon. What would you do if you were dying … *soon*."

"Well, that's easy. That would be quite a relief to know, in fact. Once you time bound an infinite game, it does in fact turn into a finite one. To be played, optimized, and conquered. All one must do is defeat the time bound."

"But that's not possible."

"And neither was getting the penny to rest, was it? Clearly, you have just shown the world that the impossible is possible. You just need to question your assumptions. It's all just physics and chemistry. So is life. So is death. So is decay. We just don't really know the rules."

"What if we did?"

"Excuse me?"

"What if we did know all the rules of decay? What if we restructured everything to play a game of DON'T DIE? Have you met Blueprint?"

"A little. Earlier, inside."

"Have you asked him about 'longevity points'?"

"He's Mormon?"

"He is decidedly *not* Mormon. But you should ask anyway."

This trick I learned from watching Cognitive Bias at work, throwing his charms all over town. I hoped that by introducing Game Play to the idea that life itself could be won, or at least turn death into a finite game, he'd stew on it for a while until 11:00 a.m. Or maybe even the rest of the day.

As if on cue, Devil May Care came out through the door just as Game Play went back inside.

Devil May Care: "This is awesome!" I only smiled. I knew if I said nothing, he'd fill in the silence like always. "The band back together!" he continued.

"It's nostalgic, that's for sure," I said.

Devil May Care: "Let's go back up the mountain. Let's do it. We barely made it last time. I hadn't even thought about it, but I still remember so fondly that first step at the summit. Who cares what we lost along the way!"

"We lost a friend," I said. "We just left him there. Just because you're over it, doesn't mean we all are, okay?"

Devil May Care: "But he didn't die! C'mon, Scribe. That was as much his choice as ours. It's possible none of us would have made it back. Instead, we all did. It all worked out." He knew my buttons. "Made a better story, too ..."

"You know what's funny, Devil May Care? Almost everyone else here, I can mentally model what they might say to a certain degree. Seeks Authority will defer to the group. Self Critical lashes out when he loses control. Cognitive Bias is a bit of a scramble, but mostly, I just need to think about one causal layer deep, and that's about where he hangs out all day. So in a strange way I don't actually miss them all that much when they're not around. Because I can imagine them. I know most of the gang so well I can sort of be with them even when we're apart. But you, sir, are P300s all day."

Devil May Care: "Pee three what now?"

"*Surprise.* You surprise my brain constantly. Three hundred milliseconds after something the brain doesn't expect, and you can see traces of the surprise in the electrical activity. In everyone's brain. And you ... with you I am always surprised. And that has two consequences. One, it makes me miss you *less* when you're not around because I can't actually rehearse what you would say in certain situations. Sure, I can remember what you've *specifically* said in the past ... that's just memory ... but I find it hard to imagine what you'll say in an imagined or new or novel scenario. So I'm mostly left with a large feeling of 'I don't know what he'd say here, but it probably pushes some limit or boundary and made someone uncomfortable,' and that keeps me from missing you because it means you show up less when I think."

Devil May Care: "I just don't do small talk. You know that." He seemed hurt, though. That wasn't my intention.

"No, I mean it in a good way," I said. "It's challenging. And useful. The most predictable person is a dead person. Literally. At every scale."

Devil May Care: "Look, I just want the group back together again and to do something *BIG.* I know you do too, Scribe. You think I'm the most relentless one, even more so than Relentless, but you know what? I think *you* are. You're the one that needs the story to last *centuries.*" He did the same twirl with his hands that Blueprint had done earlier. "Me? I'm in it for the thrill of the few seconds. I want the dopamine *now*. But you want a millennia's worth all at once, and you don't care when you get it. That's ambitious too, you know. Maybe even more so. And just as dangerous as what I do, too. Maybe even more so. You're not entirely innocent. We all push boundaries. I hop fences to get where I want to go. You move mountains to bring them to you. But we're both guilty of the same thing."

He didn't want small talk? Fine.

"If you were dying, what would you want to do most?" I asked.

Devil May Care: "I can't say that I'd do anything different than I do now. We all are dying already. Why not live that way? Are you saying you *don't* live as if you're already dying? That's irrational."

"You know what I mean. 'Sooner than expected,' I guess. I shouldn't have to define it. You understand the question."

"Truly, I don't. Let me ask you something. If you knew you were dying in forty years, would you keep doing what you're doing right now? How about ten? Five? One year? Would you?"

"Yes, I would," I said.

"And what would that be?"

"Journeying. Doing something epic. Writing my journey."

"You see. Exactly. If the thing you'd do at any of those time points is the same, don't you get it? You have already been living as if you're dying. That's great. It means you are doing what you most want at all times. It's an enviable place to be."

"Seriously, Devil May Care. What would you do if you had less than one year?"

He put his arm on my shoulder in reply.

Devil May Care: "You don't believe me, buddy, do you? I'm telling you. I would be doing exactly what I'm doing now."

I did believe him.

"Well, that's good to know," I said.

It was almost 11 a.m. I let Devil May Care know I was going inside to start the meeting, in case he wanted to be on time for once.

4: Permission Structures

Q: What is a permission structure?
Q: Who defines them?

This part would be hard for any friend group. On the dot, as an average, everyone had gathered on time. Farm Boy was exactly as early as Relentless was late. I guess it cancels out?

"Thanks everyone for coming," I said. "Many of you don't do small talk, so I'll get straight to the point. I'm dying. Today is likely my last day on this Earth."

I dismissed any small stirrings with a wave of my hand. I had learned how to perfect the gesture from the best, just a few minutes ago.

Today was not the day for wasted trivialities.

I continued, "I don't want pity. I don't want apologies. I want to live this last day to the fullest, but I am having trouble defining what that means. That's why I wanted you all here. Together, many years ago, we climbed a mountain. Now, I'll be the first to tell you that the feat alone wasn't much for the history books. Blind men have climbed Everest, which is both higher and harder. Thirty thousand people climb Kilimanjaro every year. The point is that we did it despite each other and only—*only*—because of each other. At the time, some of us were depressed. Some of us were lost. We were about to dissolve our respective marriages or our respective religions. Some of you were married to the wrong people. Some of you were wedded to the wrong God. We all had things going on bigger than the mountain. We were physically and spiritually broken, and the mountain was just a metaphor. They always are. There's no more reason to go *up* than there is to go *across* or *down* or *in*."

Model Builder tried to break through: "I can't not. What ... are you dying of?"

I stared him down.

"Do you think it hadn't occurred to me, a storyteller, whether to give the details to the most burning and obvious question in the beginning or instead to wait until the moment was right? Give me some credit, Model Builder."

Like a good stand-up comic, I had prepared for my hecklers. In fact, I needed them. Now nobody else would interrupt. Model Builder understood some things so well but some things—human things—not at all.

I continued, "Despite all these caveats, I look back at those days as some of the most important in my life. Except for Blueprint here, who is a recent friend, we were all there. It felt like if we could do that, we could do anything. People don't understand how depression can turn a molehill into a mountain. Imagine what it does to a mountain." I saw Dark Humor nod in appreciation. "It had everything. The good. The bad. The ugly. Finite struggle. Infinite reward."

Self Critical was the next heckler: "I'm usually one for speeches, but if we look over at that clock, the day is a tickin'. What's this all about, Scribe? Feels like we've already wasted half the day."

"I just wanted to ask you all a question," I said. This was it. The moment. "In person. No group chat. So that none of your units of attention, none of your attebytes are scattered across your phones and social media as half of you catch the latest viral thing. If you all could do me one last favor, it's to give all of today's attebytes to the very question I wish to now propose. Here it is."

I took a moment. Paused.

"What would you all do if you were dying today?"

After a moment, Relentless spoke up:

Relentless: "Wh—"

I interrupted, "Think about it before you speak, please. No questions. Any follow-up question is self-evident and contained within the question. You're all smart. You get it. Actually, Cognitive Bias, how about this, I'll give you a follow-up clarification question because we *all know* you have one."

That got a subdued laugh from the room.

Cognitive Bias: "Yes, I do. It seems like an impossible question, doesn't it? How can you plan for something which you have no experience with? We've never died before. Or else we wouldn't be here."

"Right, right," I said. "Good point. Touché. If it's easiest for you, how about you think of it like a counterfactual thought experiment about someone you know who did die. What do you think they wish they would have done? And then just apply that to yourself replacing the other person with 'you.' Does that work?"

Cognitive Bias: "I think so. I think so. Yeah. Yeah. I think so."

"Great," I said. "Any other questions? Any answers yet?"

Self Critical always understood people best. He got straight to the point: "Presumably, you're asking this as a prelude to the *real* question you want to ask. Can you just sort of spoiler that one for us, chap?"

"This is the only question I have for the group," I said.

Self Critical: "Hmm, I don't believe you."

"You don't need to."

"But I do have to embrace the question."

I said, "Honestly, I didn't expect you to have an answer. I expect you to answer a different question entirely. The kind of question you had wished I would have asked instead. But I do ask you this today, Self Critical, … just for today … please, just think about it and answer. How about this, everyone. To negate any biases, we all write down our answers on paper. Then we can reconvene at noon, and I'll read them aloud to the group. Sound good?"

There was no dissension among the group.

Mostly just nods.

Dark Humor: "It's quiet as a funeral here. You could hear a telomere break."

"What a perfect segue," I said. "Meet back here in a few. I'm going for a quick walk. Anyone want to join me? Seeks Authority?"

Seeks Authority: "Sure, I'll join.

A lot has changed in Seeks Authority's life lately. He seemed to be growing out of his early habits, but as we all know, those die hard. Instead of meekly following or kowtowing to the group or the group's leader, he seemed to have started to question things lately. My guess is we had time to walk the block once or twice.

Seeks Authority: "Where to?"

"How about we just walk the block once or twice?" I said.

"I prefer a goal at the end, but okay."

I knew this day was his favorite kind of gathering. In-group only. Ideally, for him that would mean no strangers. No newness. The presence of Blueprint probably made him un-easy.

I asked, "Did you meet Blueprint? I think you'd like him."

"No, not yet. Why do you think I'd like him?"

"He has a fascinating theory of group alignment. I think you'd like it. It's all about feed-forward loops and how to connect AI with human thriving. I know you like that kind of stuff."

"Interesting. I'll try to meet him. Do you like him? How did you meet?"

Old habits indeed.

"There you are again not forming your own opinions. I thought we talked about this."

Seeks Authority: "Well, I *haven't met him*. How could I have an opinion?"

"Ah, but won't my opinion of him preform your opinion even if indirectly?"

"Possibly. Fine. Never mind."

"Have you thought about the question I asked? I know it's too soon to really think it through, but I can get you back quickly enough to write down an answer."

"I already know my answer. It's easy enough to write down in time."

"Oh?"

"Yeah. 'God.' I would reconnect with God. A different one, maybe."

I stopped cold in my walk. He did too. (Of course.)

I continued, "Really? God? Why?"

"It's basic probability. *What if*? You know, there's a famous wager, Pascal's—"

"Yeah, yeah. I know. We all have Wikipedia. Can I be blunt?"

He stared at me without saying a word.

I said, "My theory? I think maybe you just want the social connections back from our childhoods. You don't want God. You want religion. You don't want to win Pascal's wager. You just want to maximize your remaining time, and you know that deep down, your happiest place is in a group of people who all believe the same thing. Secular friend groups are what, two to ten people, tops? But religious groups are in the *millions*. It's so comforting. And I too remember the feeling of approval and even when the disapproval felt so good because it came from a well-established group of authority figures. Older. Wiser. Closer to the big authority figure in the sky. Sure, the church gave themselves the authority by fiat ... but what power structure isn't by fiat these days?"

"You know, I've been thinking a lot about that lately. Where power comes from. Where permission comes from."

"Go on."

"How much time do we have? Can we try something?"

"Half an hour, maybe."

Seeks Authority: "Okay. What's the most protected place in Los Angeles?"

"Protected? What do you mean?"

"The room you need the most amount of permission to get into. Or perhaps just one permission, but it's the hardest kind to get. What do you think it would be?"

"I don't know. Some celebrity something? Some exclusive club?"

"Not even close."

"A bank vault?" I said.

I didn't see where he was going with this, honestly.

Seeks Authority: "Come on, at least try. If you tried, you'd at least come up with cleverer, less-wrong answers like the LAX control tower or the old Singer sewing machine heir's ten-bed nuclear bomb shelter. But even those are hypothetically attainable, right? For the control tower you'd just have to train to be a flight control technician or operator for a few years. Or whatever it takes. Or I bet they give tours to some flight-related people. So maybe you could buy an airline and get a tour and get your pilot friend or TSA friend to let you in. And the Singer bomb shelter I bet someone owns the house now. You could buy it or befriend them. Heck, you could even break in. The question isn't about consequences. It's about access. About permission. Sure, both of those are difficult. But they aren't impossible. There are social and permission paths to get into each of those rooms. Now think harder. Try again. What's the single room with the *hardest* permission structures to get through?"

"Honestly, I'm not sure I understand," I said.

Something had changed in Seeks Authority's voice though since I last saw him. He had an edge to him. A chip. I continued, "Doesn't the required capital or social capital make those rooms at least ... limited access? It's a matter of degree and not kind, right? Isn't money a *kind* of permission structure? For many, it is in fact the hardest one."

Seeks Authority: "So here's what I've been thinking about lately," he said, mostly ignoring my comment. "As you know, I used to defer a lot. We've talked about it. A few times. I would never choose the restaurant or the movie and just go along with the consensus. Yadda yadda. Even worse, I used to only derive joy when other people were deriving joy from situations, which ... led me to some dark places. It meant I couldn't enjoy anything when I was alone. And then when I was in a group, I didn't choose what to do. So I ended up in all kinds of places in my romantic, professional, and emotional life that I didn't thrive in. But anyway, recently, since the pandemic, I've been rethinking things. The pandemic was a remarkable control condition for permission structures. The whole society we live in was suddenly X-rayed like it never had been before. Suddenly, people who had spent their whole lives being able to afford going to hotels or on airplanes suddenly were not allowed to. Not because they ran out of money but because they ran out of access. The trappings of convenience we associate with privilege is really just a series of nested permission structures, right?"

When he emphasized certain words—*access*, *society*—he would stop walking as if the force of the thoughts was so great, they impeded his movements.

Seeks Authority: "And … it got me thinking about not just when people seek authority but about where and why the permission structures exist in the first place. Who defines them? Who cultivates and cares for them? Are they legacy structures from centuries past? And then I realized that there are in fact dozens of kinds of 'gardeners' for society—I call them 'gardeners' now, mostly for lack of a better word—who keep the hedge mazes of permissions all prim and proper. They keep us in our lanes. Tell us what can and cannot be done. It's not just lawmakers and politicians but everyone at all times. But it's a rolling boundary of course because technology often changes access and sometimes on a daily or weekly level. Let me ask you this, a related question, and we can work our way back to the permission structure question in time. Who do you think understands Los Angeles the best? Which individual *gets* it?"

"What do you mean, '*gets*' it? Gets? It?" I said. I was a bit flummoxed. But I wanted to listen to him. Seeks Authority was the best observer in the group by far from decades of being a wallflower; you learn a thing or two.

Seeks Authority: "Sure, sure. That's too easy though to dismiss the question like that. Just try. We're all playing your game in there. Play mine out here."

I said, "Okay, I *think* what you mean is who could give the most accurate bird's-eye view of why the city is the way it is? Or what it will do next? It is tricky because a civics person would say it's a bunch of cities fighting for water rights. A geologist would explain why the weather is the way it is because of the San Andreas and the fact that California is a continental shelf that could break off at any moment. A judge would say it's the penal capital of America with the largest prison system per capita. For the media, it's the entertainment capital of the world. Its hills and streets and the HOLLYWOOD sign are what most of the world pictures when they picture America, right? There's probably some newspaper reporter who has seen it all. Or some retired senator who lives a quiet life in Palos Verdes who has access to a database of every California citizen's wants, needs, income, preferences, and taxes for polling and campaign purposes. Maybe them?"

Seeks Authority: "Good, good. We're getting somewhere. Here's the thing. I actually don't know the answer to either of these questions. But what I do know is that these are questions rarely asked even though their answers are clues to the very fabric of our society. I know you like to think big, Scribe. Don't you ever stop to question why things are the way they are *now*? Pick a random time or place on this Earth and plop yourself down into any of its cities as just a normal citizen. Ancient Egypt. Modern Egypt. The Roman Empire. Sparta. Istanbul. Congo, now or then. St. Petersburg. Ancient Beijing. Feudal Japan. Māori New Zealand. There isn't just a *single* one way that it is like to be human or to run things. Every society has its own permission structures. Some are total opposites of others. So it's an almost impossible question to try to understand any one system today without understanding what the system *isn't* also. Because some of the structures are simply defined as the lack of other kinds of structures. The operating system is already written. We're just primate code sitting atop it. But at the end of the day, it feels so arbitrary, doesn't it? Perhaps a historian who won't even be born until 2,500 will be the person who best understands this dreadful town."

"I have a feeling you're about to tell me that this isn't actually about Los Angeles, is it?" I asked. I knew sometimes he needed the listener to guide the twist.

Seeks Authority stopped walking.

Smiled.

He knew.

Seeks Authority: "Oh, I missed you, Scribe. Nothing gets past you. No, of course this isn't about LA. It's about the society of mind. The society of body. Control. Capital. Which part of me has control? Who defines the alignments between our organs, our bodies, our interests, and our mind? Why can't I tell my stubbed toe to stop hurting? Or my paper cut to stop bleeding? Isn't it *my* body? Is a mind just one thing or is it a bunch of incorporated regions with energy and land rights disputes who secretly hate their neighbors and who barely add up to more than a sum of their individual parts?"

"I get it. What you want to know is, who sets the permission structures for my conscious decisions?"

"Exactly. Well, not just that. Recently, I entirely stopped listening to my conscious mind."

"*What?* What does that even mean?"

"It means that once I took true stock of the permission structures that run my body and mind, I was able to ask a few real questions. Which part of me understands the whole the best? And if no one part does, who do I trust? Do I trust the immediacy and reward of a late-night craving for cake just sitting in the fridge like a temptress? Or do I hold off for some sort of long-term ideal of better sleep, weight, fitness, and health? Do I prioritize social interaction now or deep sleep tonight for tomorrow's unknown gauntlet of activity? Is my future self the final arbiter of all decisions? It's got a sort of Zeno's paradox to it, doesn't it? If I'm always meeting Future Self halfway, did I ever really decide anything *for me*?"

"What does the conscious mind have to do with this?" I asked.

"It's an alignment issue. It's a society of mind issue. A permissions structure issue. The conscious mind is used to not having to ask permission. It just sits there, like a God-king, thinking what it thinks and shaping behaviors and preferences for some unspoken, poorly understood goal that may or may not be reproduction, but it's not like it'll ever just *tell you that*, will it?"

"It does, though. That's what preferences *are*. That's what decisions *are*."

"Look, the year of Kilimanjaro I was depressed. *Depressed*. I had terrible discipline around diet. My conscious brain was lighting up all the wrong things. Late-night cookies, comfort foods. Each too tempting for my weakened brain. These sugary objects were being artificially lit up by some broken wires. We should even ask Cognitive Bias about it. He's into pop psychology. Maybe it's a thing. Who knows? All I know is that they were not good for me. These seductive objects were the brightest when I was darkest. One thing I did recently was to make my smartphone black and white. You ever do that? It means the apps are less good at controlling when you attend to them. You can take back just a tiny dreg of control. And I thought, 'What if I could make my decision-making and cognition monochrome?' No more Technicolor, brightly lit, bad decisions. How did I do it, you ask? You'll like this. I became a Mormon Lucifer. I've noticed a few years ago that some people, even in our group—Dark Humor, Self Critical, and you sometimes, if I'm being honest—have started to blame algorithms for their behaviors as if it wasn't them. Wrong. Wrong. Wrong. *You* are late to the dinner party. Not the AI taxi. *You*. It's like blaming your shoe for being late because it came untied. Wrong. This is quite a slippery slope because it means that people have started to incorporate algorithms into their lives and decisions, but on the flip side, they don't take personal responsibility for them when everything goes belly up. It *feels* like a win-win, at first … you always get an excuse for every social faux pas? Sign me up. But is it, really?"

"I have to say, Seeks Authority, I really love this new you. And, just to reiterate, you have to talk to Blueprint. Seriously."

"I will. I will. So but I have started to think that this 'alignment' problem between humans and their own minds is *the* existential question of our time. Evolution did not prepare us for the modern world. We are too tempted. Always. Personally, I have a catastrophic and seemingly irreconcilable goal alignment problem within myself. Who's in charge and when? And how is that question/conflict to be resolved? Recently I put my conscious mind into purgatory, and I don't regret it for a second. I don't have to ask it for permission anymore. I don't need its approval.

It was one of the best decisions of my life and has yielded rapid gains. It reminded me of the beginning of my decades of depression when I learned that an endless stream of thoughts and emotions expressing hopelessness was not *me* but something else spewing bile onto my conscious existence. If I had listened to those thoughts, they would have chartered me on a path toward self-destruction and suicide. I doubt I would still be here.

We both grew up in a small, rural town in Utah … what was it, 99.9 percent Mormon? Out of thirty thousand? That's a lot of town-wide alignment. Mormonism was the only reality I knew existed, and in that belief system nothing exceeds the conscious mind in importance. Free will is the single vector to recognize truth and the path to eternal salvation. It is everywhere in the foundational elements of Mormon mythology. All non-Mormons, I was taught, were wrong in thought and belief and needed to be converted in order to be saved.

And what's the myth? The story Mormons tell everyone from before they can even babble? That one day, God decided to test his children to determine their eternal salvation by championing a plan where each of us humans would be endowed with free will, a physical body, and seventy-ish years of dreary life on Earth. And in that life, we could either choose to accept or reject his commandments—using, of course, just a bunch of arbitrary sets of emotions, sensors, cognitive biases, and social rules that he himself *also* gave us, probably as a kind of handicap—that would give some entry into eternal salvation.

But, as the story is told, Lucifer, like a board member, offered an alternative plan: What if everyone would still receive a body and live a great life on Earth and they would all achieve eternal salvation because none of them would have *free will* to mess it up? Because then *everyone* would get in, right? God of course rejected the plan and cast him out forever. Using, you guessed it, *free will* to decide, right? Sort of useful when he has it, huh? And now we humans, inheritors of all this debate, swear up and down the world over that we would choose choice. But really, maybe Lucifer was kind of onto something?

If success or failure in life and eternal salvation hinges upon human ability to exercise free will and exert self-control, then doesn't this also include obeying all of God's commandments and not eating that brightly lit sugar cookie? Growing up, think about all the rules we had. Is it really free will if it is so constrained all the time? No coffee. No alcohol. It's not a chill religion, Scribe. It was kind of algorithmic, come to think of it. Why give will in the first place if you're just going to constrain it?"

It was nearing noon, but I had to say something. Ironically, I felt both compelled and free to.

I said, "I need to think this through for a while, Seeks Authority. I'm compelled, but what I worry about is whether or not what you're saying generalizes. What it sounds like is that you don't trust *your* conscious mind. That it has tricked you in the past with religion and depression, and the only logical conclusion is that it may still be tricking you.

But also, historically, you always hated making decisions, didn't you? That was part of the whole intervention we had with you years back when we trained you how to speak up for yourself and stop deferring. So we're almost back, but I want to say that I love parts of this. But you should ask yourself whether this is just a logical solution to hating making decisions.

Nobody really *likes* making tough decisions. It's extremely rare to actually care what food the group eats, but ultimately a decision must be made. There are consequences, and sometimes they are unknown or scary, but there is beauty in that too. One knows that one has changed the world in a causal way. Whether it's a mistake or a reward, *something* changed. That's what life is. That's what we're here for ... to impact things. To change things. That's all we can do. Also, if you don't find Blueprint, I'm going to kidnap both of you and sit you down together, I promise. It feels like the most important thing I might ever do, connecting you two."

When we arrived back at the house the door was open. Everybody was inside the living room silently waiting for us. Dark Humor was right.

It was like a funeral in here.

5: Seriously,
What Would You Do If You Were Dying?

Seriously, though...
Q: What would you do?

Everyone had written down their answers and put them in a bowl except Seeks Authority, who just before he sat down took one answer out, ripped off a small corner from it, wrote 'God,' showed it to the room, and put both back in the bowl.

"Thank you, everyone," I said. "Let's just get to it, shall we? I already know some answers from brief conversations I've had with a few of you, but I'll still read them out so the group knows, too. Now of course this is an exercise I've already done, and you already know my answer. My answer is this." I used the grand gesture again. "My answer is this meeting, today. I'm being as honest as I can here. If I was dying, I would want to first write a book widely read centuries from now. Now let's see what else we got."

I randomly picked another answer from the bowl.

"Self Critical says, 'If I was dying, I would want to first punish myself thoroughly for all misdeeds. Atone.'"

Again I picked.

"Devil May Care says, 'If I was dying, I would want to first make up for lost time.' Great. On-brand. I suspect everyone here will be on-brand."

Another.

"Relentless says, 'If I was dying, I would want to first have an epic plan for death and leave the world by saving it.' I like that one. Save the world. Humble."

"Seeks Authority says, 'If I was dying, I would first to God.' Okay, not a complete sentence, but we get it, I think."

"Yep," said Seeks Authority.

Half the room nodded in surprise at his answer.

Two people at once—I couldn't tell who—in synchrony start up:

"Wait..."

"Wait..."

"Not now," I said. "Let's wait."

I picked another.

"Cognitive Bias says, 'If I was dying, I would want to first make sure my kids are taken care of and rewrite the deathbed ritual and rites.' I like that, CB. Let's make sure to go back to that."

And another.

"Blueprint says, 'If I was dying, I would want to first stop it.' Of course you would, Blueprint. *Of course* you would say that."

And another.

"Model Builder says, 'If I was dying, I would want to first race toward completing the mission.'" I paused, as if to ask Model Builder with my glare, *And what mission would that be, exactly?* But I said nothing.

And another.

"Farm Boy says, 'If I was dying, I would want to first write gratitude notes to everyone who has been a positive force in my life.' Love it, FB. Love it."

And another.

"Now, this next one is Game Play's. He and I already spoke about this outside, so let's see if he says the same thing. Game Play says, 'If I was dying, I would want to, first …' I don't actually understand this, Game Play. All it says is, 'RECONCILIATION DEATH PROCESS' in capital letters. Can you explain?"

Game Play: "It's from *Arrival*, the movie. I love that movie. The creatures don't seem to have a word for 'dying.' They just say 'death process' like it's an annoying action that must be carried out in the morning like taking a bath or unloading the dishwasher or flossing. 'Excuse me, nurse, could you please facilitate death process, perhaps with some opiates?' That sort of thing. So basically, I would want to either emotionally or physically reconcile with the death process. Understand it. What does a body really die of? I've never quite understood a coroner's reports on death and dying. One doesn't die of anything other than oxygen deprivation, right? That's the proximate cause of all death? So we're just working back from a few seconds of hypoxia, no matter what anyone says. Even when the dinosaurs got hit by an asteroid or someone was thrown into a volcano in some barbaric Mesoamerican ritual, they died because not enough oxygen made it to their brain at the microsecond level."

Blueprint: "That's not strictly speaking true."

Game Play: "Oh? Do tell, doctor."

Blueprint: "I'm not a doctor," said Blueprint.

And another.

The last in the bowl.

"Later, later, gentleman," I intervened. "Last but not least we have Dark Humor. Anyone want to guess what Dark Humor said?"

Dark Humor: "Do a stand-up routine in front of my children and one million other people."

I said, "Okay, sure. Yes, you guessed your own answer correctly, Dark Humor. Well done."

"Thank you."

"Did anyone notice something in common across all these answers? Anything at all?" I asked.

Dark Humor, flatly: "They are lies."

"Say more, please," I said.

Dark Humor: "Yours seems to be the only honest answer, Scribe. But even then, I detect a hint of duplicity. You said two things. One, you'd want a gathering of your closest friends. And second, you'd write a book that would still be read centuries from now. But I don't see you slaving over a pen and paper right now, which means either you weren't telling the truth about the latter one or probably you've combined the two in your heart. In other words, the only reasonable conclusion we should arrive at is that *you are gathering us here today to write your book*. And I suspect some of the other answers were also shortcuts.

Me, for example. I don't actually want to do stand-up in front of one million people. I want to *have been* someone who had *already* done stand-up in front of one million people and for it to be widely known such that even Barnum has to turn over the trademark, and on the last day of life I would sit and relive those glorious memories over and over with my kids nearby until I made them genuinely laugh. It's genuine laughter from my children that I prize more than anything in this life or any other."

Dark Humor had a point. I forgot how well this group knew me. And how well some of them knew themselves and each other.

Game Play stood up to speak: "Let me ask the group what you asked me outside, Scribe. It's sort of like a follow-up question. Or an amendment to the question. Is there anyone here whose answer would change depending on the time-scale? What if you knew you were dying in forty years? Ten? Five? One? What about one month? Or tomorrow? Scribe's question was intentionally vague, I believe, to ignore time-scales. We all presumed our own, but I just want to clarify which we each chose. Raise your hands. Who would change their answer if the timescale changed?"

At that, Game Play raised his hand.

Only one other hand went up: Blueprint.

Game Play: "Great. Blueprint, you first, if you don't mind. Why would you change your answer?"

Blueprint: "Because the technology of death—the death process—is changing. In the eighteenth century what counted as death was different than in the nineteenth, which was different than in the twentieth. Every decade seems to bring with it new advances that increase longevity. Let's say that dying has units. Let's just call them 'longevity points' for now since I know a few of you here are familiar with that language. Okay, so the question is: If longevity units are a kind of currency, can you apply economic forecasting models to the currency over time with concepts like inflation, leveraging, and the like? I think you can. And I believe that longevity points will be worth more the farther into the future we go because of both structural and natural inflation. To truly understand the question then, one must consider all of its variables. The very premise of the question requires that we choose from a single vantage—today—that is, from our points of view right now. But to answer the question at its heart, I believe we must instead use a kind of rolling version of identity and ask ourselves about the dynamically changing nature of the future. Here's the TL;DR: I believe that we are at an inflection point and that forty years is *very* different from ten in terms of longevity. So I would prioritize different things, yes, depending on the timescale of the answer."

Self Critical: "Who the hell mentioned longevity? You seem to be assuming that a well-lived life, regardless of its duration, is irrelevant? This isn't about duration. It's about quality. I don't want to live any longer in *this* life."

Yes, he used the grand gesture. I guess we all learned it from each other.

Blueprint fired back: "Well, you have to be alive to live *any* kind of life, good or bad. The point is that there is a kind of 'escape velocity'—the idea is not mine—for mortality, and if you were to create a nested hierarchy of problems for first solving meaning and purpose, you'd of course need to know how long you were going to live. And the longer, the better. Why not? How could it not be? Otherwise, why continue at all with the time we have? We can talk about it also as an almost artistic matter if you'd like. What we're asking about is the size of the canvas we want to paint on. We will splatter it with paint later. But we need to know the size of the canvas to know the size of the ambition of the painting. Which, by analogy, represents the life we wish to live. A bigger canvas allows for different kinds of paintings. Epic ones. It's not a matter of degree with canvas size. It's a matter of kind. I, for example, in the last year have reversed many key measures of aging. I stretched my extra canvas."

Self Critical: "*Key measures*? Of *aging*? Before I say more, I'd actually love for you to go on because I suspect you'll do my counterargument for me without realizing it."

Model Builder: "Can I just say one thing first? Something I've never understood but I promise is relevant to this little debate you two are having. The way I understand it, you two are arguing about time in a broad sense. But it's not really just one thing because different parts of the body have different clocks. Of course, we all know that different organisms have different life spans. Dragonflies live twenty-four hours. Cuttlefish live one year, tops. Mice a few years. We wouldn't dare even ask what it would mean for a human to live a good life if life was only twenty-four hours long. But our bodies are not just one thing. We have dragonflies within us. We have cuttlefish within. What I mean is that we have some cells that turn over extremely rapidly like endothelial cells and some that never do like neurons. We're not just one thing. We're not just one age. And here's the amazing thing that I don't understand but seems relevant—*there is no tree ring for age*.

"There are clues within ranges like bone densities and growth and jaw and tooth placements, but for the most part, there is *no way at all* to determine how old someone is. There was even a case in New York a while back of a suspected Somali pirate who the US wanted to charge but didn't know if he was a kid or an adult. He had no idea when he was born. There's not exactly a paper trail where he was from. His dad claimed one age. His mom, another. Nobody knew. And the best minds in modern biological science sure didn't either. So my question to you, Blueprint, is, how do you know you 'reversed' your age according to these key measures without a tree ring?"

Dark Humor: "That's a good point. If you did your magic to a tree, Blueprint, would we see the rings disappear?"

Blueprint: "I don't want to derail things just yet." He flushed a little from the attention. "There are markers. Epigenetic clocks. There are many kinds depending on the scientist or the focus. I can go into them sometime if anyone is interested, but my general point is that usually one can slow down these markers of aging. But the hoped-for gold standard holy grail, of course, would be to *reverse them*. We are seeing some exciting reversals. But I don't want to belabor that point with Scribe here barely having, what is it, a single day left?"

"Yes, true. I'm the dragonfly now," I said.

The room went silent.

I continued, "Don't be dour, friends. Dark Humor is right. I *want* to write that book, but obviously I don't have the time to. That's my first lesson, I suppose. The best time to plant a tree is twenty years ago, but the next best time is today, right? If you truly know the answer to your question, do that thing now. Today. But this isn't that kind of day. This isn't about regret. The question I'm pondering is the extent to which it's okay to keep going and the limits on what I can ask of myself and those around me. My question—forgive me, as I know we are nearing lunch—is about the ethics of self-harm. This is my simple question: If my hand was gangrenous, and I would die unless I cut it off, *should I*?" A few immediately stood up at the visceral-ness of the question or hid their head in, ironically, their hands. It hit some like a hot, hard wind, as if what I said riled their defenses like the presence of a real threat in the room would have. "No need to be so defensive. I'm sorry for the surprise. This is still and will always be about the group's decision-making."

Relentless: "What sadist would ask such a thing?"

He walked over and held one of my hands in his. As if to protect it.

Devil May Care: "This is no game?"

"It is not a game," I said.

Devil May Care: "Can you explain the details? I don't understand."

Game Play: "I mean, I see what this is. Don't be fooled, everybody. This is the same thought experiment made real. Made corporeal. The question is still about the quality of a life versus its duration. Does one live longer for the sake of longer alone? What is it acceptable to sacrifice in the meantime or to ensure it? Blueprint, you would say an automatic yes to this diseased hand-for-one-life exchange, right? Of course *you* think it's worth it. In fact, many of us would think so if we were trapped outdoors under a boulder and the only way to survive would be to gnaw off a limb. It's instinct to keep going. It's easy to frame that story because the universe of cause and effect forced us into a corner. Animals would do it in a heartbeat to make sure they still had a heartbeat. It's survival. Of course we have an instinct to try to survive as long as possible, whatever the cost. It's built into us all somewhere. Truly, whatever the cost. Just because the terms are made clearer and there isn't a boulder in the way shouldn't change the morality or the calculation. I vote: *Do it*."

There was so much commotion and so many voices I couldn't keep track of who said what anymore: "There's a clear difference, though. This is a decision made by a conscious self, offering the trade. It's horrible." / "Boulder or belief system. What's the difference if you're trapped beneath it?" / "Scribe is not trapped. That's the difference." / "But he is, in a sense? Right, Scribe?"

"Yes, that is right, whoever said that. I die at midnight," I said.

"There's a huge difference. A boulder can't be moved. A person can." / "A constrained life is just as worth living." / "Nobody is tracking dexterity quotients here and especially not in the end. Nobody on their deathbed says they wish they had more degrees of freedom. They say they wish they spent more time relaxing or by themselves or with loved ones. In purely utilitarian terms, if you believe a life is worth living, a life *must* go on if you have the choice." / "We are all constrained. Think about how advanced technology will be centuries from now. Our brains of today will be thought of as puny illiterates. Constrained. And yet we persist. Do we think the life of a human living forty thousand years ago was somehow less worth living despite its constraints? What is the difference between a hand and kinds of cognition?"

The room blew up. It became a cacophony.

"This isn't about optimizing. This is about the ethics of self-harm." / "But we know this dilemma well. Kilimanjaro. We left behind Depression so we could all survive. That's no different. We cut the hand off the group, didn't we?"

The room got quiet for a few moments until it exploded again.

I closed my eyes to try to hear everyone.

"That wasn't the same. He chose to stay." / "The naturalness of the causality *does* matter. If Scribe is dying under natural circumstances and the promised intervention is an unnatural one, it is the same as the boulder situation. We've seen this movie, *127 Hours*. It wouldn't be a movie unless the guy made the correct decision." / "It's a movie *precisely because* he made an unpopular and unnatural decision. We don't film people doing everyday acts of everyday morality and expect people to pay for the privilege of watching it."

I called for the room's silence.

"This is not a trick question," I said. "I promise. I'm trying to weigh all options. Can I ask everyone to think about how different the question is to, say, the common choice to do chemotherapy? Isn't that also a kind of intentional and massive harm to the body at various scales, all and exclusively for the sake of survival? What are the limits of acceptable self-harm for the sake of life itself within an individual? I have, by the way, already chosen my answer. It is: no. Today is my last day. Please do not ask why or any more questions about it. What I would like though is for us to get to the next part of the day with your personal answers to these questions in mind. Because these are the foundational topics for the matter *that is really* at hand. *We need to do something epic.* That's my psychology but also my request. I can't do it alone in less than a day. I need you all. And my premise is this: I'm not the only one dying. So is the planet. So is Earth. And so are we all. So are you all. Humanity is hurtling toward its own self-wrought extinction. If you need a metaphor—this is mostly for you, Game Play—and if humanity's time on this planet were a sport, well, then it's halftime, and we're getting our asses kicked. How do we change that?"

Game Play: "This is the huddle."

"Exactly," I said. "This is the huddle. And we know the stakes. So ... does anyone have a plan?"

Seeks Authority: "I think I get it. Humanity has less than twenty-four hours left, figuratively. Probably a few centuries at the going pace, but you're making it by analogy to an individual's life in order to make the point about how dire things are for all of humanity. The question being, 'What should we do with the time left?'"

Relentless: "And, specifically, we need to use our answer to the amount of acceptable self-harm required to keep going. Whether to cut our hand off or irradiate the most toxic cells. You all know my vote there. I do everything mostly for the thrill alone. Self-preservation is vastly inferior to hedonic experience or experience itself in my hierarchy of needs. I'm in, Scribe. Whatever you need."

"Alas, that's the problem," I responded. "I don't know what is needed. All I know is that we solved Kilimanjaro as a team and that if we solve the alignment problem between the lot of us, we will easily be able to make a plan. And what I hope for is that the plan generalizes such that the structures of the alignments themselves—here perhaps they are restricted to psychological and between us, but out there we need alignment between all systems at all scales. Between humans and each other. Between humans and our technology, including AI. Between our technology and our entire world. Outside this room I am shocked at how rarely I hear about a plan."

Self Critical: "Perhaps because not everybody has the need, means, or interest in solving the world. It's a luxurious contemplation exercise. The Prada stamp for the catalog of thought exercises. Mostly people spend their time solving the needs of their day, their week, or their month. What have future generations ever done for us?"

Game Play: "That's not a criticism. That's simply one part of one variable in the multidimensional alignment problem. A realistic constraint for any plan, especially a grand one that requires all kinds of mobilizations, is a consideration for who has the means or interest. And we can define 'means' and 'interest' in many ways. 'Means' can be time, money, metabolism, attebytes, anything. Some have excessive wealth, but their thoughts are worse than nothing. Some have exquisite thoughts and no financial or metabolic means. Some can devote all of their daily attebytes. Some only a few or none. This is *part* of the alignment problem, not its death knell."

Farm Boy: "I agree."

This was a rare occurrence.

"Go on," I said, hoping to encourage him.

Farm Boy: "As I sat here listening, I realized how ill-suited I am to this day and really to this task. If I was told humanity had one hundred years, I would spend as much as I could with my family and loved ones. Keep them close. Live simply on my farm and hope my children do the same."

"Au contraire, Farm Boy," I said. "There is nobody here whose voice and creativity are not a key piece to the puzzle. We *will* need your bucolic humility in the future, Farm Boy. Relentless over here forgets there even *are* rural parts of America. Game Play doesn't know how to give units to 'contentment,' and without a unit of measurement he can't run his minimax or Monte Carlo routines. To him, satiety, love, and goodness are

NP-hard problems, for heaven's sake. But I see no reason from first principles why a possible solution won't require a perspective just like Farm Boy's."

Game Play: "You mean from zeroth principles."

"No, I mean from *first*. Zeroth-principled thinking is *your* wacky idea. I've never quite understood it."

Blueprint: "I read up on some of Game Play's ideas. I like them. Quite a bit. The concept of starting with zero has informed many of my team's assumptions about how the human body works. It's been a revelation to step back."

Model Builder: "I haven't caught up. Someone care to explain?"

"Not yet," I said. "We don't need it now. Zeroth-principled thinking is a methodological tool for arriving at new ideas and possible solutions when we seem stuck. We're not stuck yet. In fact, we haven't even started."

6: The Autonomous Body

Q: Is automation good?
Q: Is it the end of free will?

In many ways this was the moment I had been rehearsing in my head for the past few months, both excitedly and dreading, in equal measure. "Blueprint," I said, "could you introduce yourself more to the group? I've been wanting you all to meet for a while now. I know some of you have met him today, but there's more to Blueprint than just UV monitors and diet tricks, I promise. Could you perhaps explain what you've been up to the last few years? Just the basics. Maybe start with the Autonomous Self? Or maybe somewhere a bit easier like the Autonomous Body?"

Model Builder: "Most of our body is *already* autonomous."

"I know, I know," I replied. "Just. Listen. Please. For me."

Self Critical: "You can only play that card so many times today, Scribe."

Relentless: "I envy Scribe, in a way. Today is pretty much the only day where he can ignore anything you say, Self Critical. All day. Have you ever noticed your criticisms are always about the future or the past? They are never about the present."

Dark Humor chimed in: "Wait, so if we're all just mostly autonomous machines, does that mean I can leave, and nobody will hold it against me? Because you can't blame me, right, if my conscious mind didn't choose to because how could I choose not ... to?"

Everyone in the room recognized a Dark Humor bluff when they saw one.

Blueprint stood up instead of responding directly.

Blueprint, introducing himself: "Hi, all. Okay, so, yes, Model Builder, you are correct that *most* of our body is autonomous. But it is not aligned. There is no one superordinate goal that the individual parts of the body all have. Truly there's not a single one. Not even 'stay alive' or 'reproduce' or any of the simple ones most people think of. There are too many cells and too many systems for each of them to understand and share the goal. Many cells stay alive long after a body dies. We are really not just one thing. Many of our organ systems do not even communicate with each other, or if they do, they do so barely at all. There's an ancient network of aqueducts in all of us carrying hormones and chemical signals everywhere, but not only do we not fully understand the communication protocols between our organ systems or within any single organ system, we have very little ability to do anything about it even if we *could* listen in.

"Imagine a visit to a heart doctor. They might say something like, 'Your cholesterol is a bit high, so I'm going to need you to begin exercising'? Which is of course good advice, but it's shorthand. It is a *kind* of automated deferral of willpower to a folk algorithm that says in simple terms that if cholesterol is 'high,' to stop doing things that we know that make it higher. In the cardiologist's case we have an expert human in the decision-making loop, but they are operating off of population averages, studies, and their best guesses in the guise of intuition. The goal of the Autonomous Body is to have no humans in the decision-making loop. So these last few years have been a journey of mine not to *supplant* the body's natural mechanisms but to enhance them with the right kind of data. I believe that we are at the beginning here. We are just beginning to understand how to program the human body. An entirely new and previously undetected organ system, some transit system attached to our intestines, was discovered *in the last decade.* An entire human organ! Seriously! That's like discovering a new planet right in our backyard.

"And so for about the past two years I have been working with top physicians, scientists, and technologists with the goal of adding a layer of automation to my body and mind. Today I methodically track hundreds of biomarkers each day in order to measure all seventy organ systems and use my body as a vehicle for extreme health experimentation. The goal is to push the boundaries of what we know about *why* a body breaks down, which starts with being able to predict *when.*"

Model Builder: "So this system would be like high-frequency trading but for organs? For nutrients and metabolites?"

Blueprint: "I'm not sure I get that analogy right away. Could you explain that, Model Builder?"

Model Builder: "Sure. In a sense, the history of some economic transactions can be told as the story of a series of moves toward autonomy. Direct bartering at some point became mediated by money, which then stood as a symbolic proxy for those goods until almost like a global, coherent language we started being able to manipulate just the symbols alone. And then at some point we made algorithms to interact with all the markets, and now we mostly just transfer digital bits around between each other, markets, and banks. Last year we had almost nine trillion dollars of digital transactions globally. The end goal for making wise decisions within these markets created the need for a kind of algorithmic and automated arms race for both data bandwidth and speed. Hence, high-frequency trading, which happens at speeds way too quick for human perception or decision-making because the markets can change in nanoseconds.

"And so you seem to be saying, Blueprint, if I hear you right, that something similar could happen one day with our bodies? The idea being that right now when the body itself determines the dietary, nutritional, or health outcomes it most desires, it actually doesn't have the right data or a complete view of what the rest of the body is concerned with. And so if we can intervene at a very specialized layer in the global decision-making of a body's health and wellness, my guess is that the system would work a bit like the high-frequency trading bots, which are mostly autonomous, intervene at a subhuman layer in the economy, and which can move entire markets in seconds. Here the 'market' would of course be some standard of health or care or whatever the individual most values."

Self Critical: "This all seems quite unnatural. Our bodies are not markets."

Blueprint was nonplussed. I knew he was used to hearing the low-hanging criticisms. He told me once that he knew from experience to not ever get defensive but to instead walk people slowly through the new ideas. Blueprint, softly: "We will have to confront the idea of 'natural' carefully. Homeostasis—in the analogy this would be, say, market stability—is naturally fragile. Let's think through, for example, what we naturally have control over our own bodies. As you all were climbing Mt. Kilimanjaro, did you consider the elaborate mechanistic steps for breathing and the strange fact that individuals do not ever once think about breathing if they don't wish to? But with just a little exertion of will or a kind push from a Sherpa or a single repetitive meditation mantra we can also breathe at our own pace. So we have a weird kind of hybrid system where the automation can be switched on and off literally at will.

"But some things in our bodies we cannot control. This is to your brilliant point earlier, Model Builder. I see your trading floor analogy now. When we stub our toe, we cannot turn off the pain. If we're bleeding, we can't coordinate immune or clotting factors to come in and staunch the wound. If we're in pain, we can't release the body's natural morphine to quell the storm or

73

time the peak of its effect. These are all happening below human perceptual thresholds, just like the international markets. They are impossible to keep track of.

"Immediately this brings to mind many questions. *Who* made the natural trade-offs in our bodies? When do we get access to this logic, if ever? Why can we control *some* but not all bodily processes? Are they running efficiently? How can we know? Where is the board of directors for bodily decisions located in the body or mind? What is the ideal balance between automation and free will? Against what tyranny can we protest in rage to regain our freedoms of choice?

"Think just about the food we will have shortly for lunch. The decision authority about what to eat and when has always rested with the conscious mind and the vague emotional drives driven by some part of the body's desired biochemical state. The currency of this decision authority was the biochemical processes. Mostly there was some top-down control, like the Federal Reserve, making sure global systems stay within expected ranges. But what I've been working on for a while now is letting the organs and biological processes be in charge. They can use their own currencies to consummate transactions on *their* terms. Instead of a doctor playing with population averages and hunches from generations-old medical training, my liver tells me what it needs through a simple readout. It gets a vote. It doesn't follow RDAs or serving sizes. It speaks directly to the Blueprint in the sky, so to speak. Our job from the outside is to get the best and most reliable data. The biomarkers we need are data nestled in gold-standard scientific evidence."

Model Builder stood up and started pacing. The entire room could tell his mind was racing in proportion to his feet. Blueprint seemed to intuit that it was worth waiting for him to speak first before continuing.

Model Builder: "Okay, so, let's work with this. Premise one, which everybody knows is on the horizon, is that almost everything in the future will be programmable. If the twentieth century was the century of programmable physics—the atom, silicon, and so on—then the twenty-first century is the century of programmable biology. This will be true from individual molecules to organs all the way up through societal governance and belief systems. I've seen behind the curtain at a few of these companies lately, and recent progress in science and engineering makes it clear that food, energy, molecules, and organs are being broken apart and recombined at the atomic and molecular level and that this trend will soon trickle up, too. Germline genome engineering is way too slow. I'm talking about engineering the cells as they live, breathe, and die. Live. Daily. Their proteins and chemistry and membranes. Every building block of life will be programmable. And eventually we will have a kind of object-oriented programming for biology that intervenes at the organ or system level. It is easy to then imagine that, as more of the software becomes algorithmic, society will too as decisions get stripped away from us more and more. We can get a rough estimate of the progress of such velocity from how quickly during just the last decade alone AI has become part of the decision-making loop for almost all aspects of society and governance. Advertising, purchasing, banking, law, medicine, manufacturing, transportation, and city planning—all are AI driven these days. That's just the start. It's everywhere now. Almost literally everywhere.

He continued: "So, if I may skip ahead a bit, Blueprint, with where I see your idea is leading you, you are saying that the kinds of work you are doing now on bodily and mental health will one day become relevant at the scale necessary for individual and species-level survival. But before we get there, we must solve the simpler problems like the alignment between an individual and their own body and mind. And that once we get that down we can move on to bigger and bigger projects at every scale, including the relationship between humanity and a peacefully coexisting AI or between humanity and the worst of itself or between all life, artificial or biological, and our shared environment, all under one roof together."

Blueprint: "Bravo, Model Builder. I keep a highly detailed log of all my statistical and methodological errors, like an explorer's log, which must include as many wrong moves and all the right ones too. I believe that this is the foundation of, as Scribe might call it, a Plan. *The* Plan."

Cognitive Bias: "What's the alignment problem? Like, alignment with tires? Which reminds me I should probably do that soon. Anyone know a good local mechanic?"

Blueprint: "No, no. Much harder than aligning tires. The challenge, sometimes called the 'goal-alignment problem,' is a concept from AI research where some programmers noticed that software programs sometimes end up performing in ways that surprise their creators. Given a narrow set of goals or a misprogrammed alignment, homeostatic loops can get out of whack very quickly. A couple years ago, there was an AI that embedded information in otherwise dead pixels to cheat at a classification task its creators gave it. They weren't specific enough in telling the AI what its goals were. Misalignment can go very wrong very quickly. And that's kids' play, just a silly experiment. But misalignment can go all the way up. One of the US military's earliest autonomous jets used exclusively digital circuit boards and figured out how to short its own circuits to run some analog calculations, which massively surprised its programmers. Such surprises can happen for many reasons, but often it is because the initial programmed goals were not made clear enough or did not account for all the complex possibilities of interaction with the real world. Goal alignment is thus essential to the relationship between humanity and to all automated systems. Who cares if everything is programmable if the programs are not working for *us*?

"We are already living in an increasingly autonomous age, with a slow erosion of human decision-making. All systems tend toward autonomy with the trend always removing the human from the decision or operations loop. The ways that people describe their relationship to automated systems is evolving as well. The problem is that this has mostly happened without full ethical or causal considerations—considerations that we must take up if we are to try to solve the biggest and thorniest problems we face like climate change or efficient global or local governance. The driving hypothesis of my work is that each kind of automation will follow the same general trajectory as all the others but just at different scales. In other words, the lessons learned from the Autonomous Body are scaled up to meet the demands and constraints of solving global problems like our planet's metabolic health as a whole. And one day, I can imagine the world's oceans, atmosphere, and some sort of homeostatic range will be tracked to the same accuracy and precision that one's bodily measurements could be today. The Earth has to balance its extraordinarily complex biosphere just as our body has to fight to achieve balance in what it lords over. It's all the same. Systems balancing themselves."

I interrupted, "This reminds me of what the mathematician and philosopher A.N. Whitehead once said, that civilizations advance by extending the number of important operations that we can perform without thinking about them."

Relentless seemed excited—he too paced when excited, and you could almost see his pupils dilate: "This is great. Just great. So we can start to imagine an existence where cognitive biases are eliminated as much as possible. Where harmful health and personal decisions are avoided through data like with traffic and weather. Where humans, AI, and the planet exist in support of each other rather than in opposition. And where the future is less than totally unknowable because we are, in a sense, its engineers. And that in order to confront the existential risks and pitfalls of the future, we will need to transmute as many metabolic, cognitive, and environmental efforts we currently worry ourselves with into those that we can perform without thinking about them. Like you said about Whitehead."

Blueprint: "Precisely. What we need to progress is the demotion of the conscious mind and the elevation of autonomous systems for decision-making too complex for the human mind to consider. People protested seatbelts, medical masks, you name it. People will protest. It's what they do. This has happened before, and it will happen again. Each of us experiences reality as though it were the first time this thing has ever happened when in reality it's happened dozens, hundreds, thousands, or even billions of times before. People's response to progress in automation is influenced by their life experiences and perceptual pattern matching, which evolution uses to keep us vigilant and alarmed."

Model Builder was so excited to speak he was almost agitated: "Maybe we could even come up with something akin to Moore's law, which is, for those who don't know, the observation that the number of transistors that can fit on a computer chip will double every year. Maybe there is an analogous law for the progress of autonomous systems. We can call it 'Whitehead's law.' The idea being that things always tend *toward* rather than away from automation. But how fast? I think it is safe to say that, roughly, for a given system, there seems to be a halving of manual operations required for a human per decade. Or, thought of in the inverse, the rate of new operations one can perform without thinking about them will *double approximately every decade.*

Blueprint: "In fact you may even be able to tell the whole century-long story of automobiles and human behavior in terms of Whitehead's law and its gradual encroachment on free will. There's your book, Scribe."

"Excuse me?" I said.

Self Critical: "Pop psychology, nothing more. Isn't applying a concept from physics and mapping it onto basic psychology the alchemical formula for nonfiction ideas these days? Half these books are just a single metaphor with anecdotes dangling like Christmas ornaments off of their line breaks."

Model Builder: "But we might actually be onto something here. As cars became more sophisticated, computerized, and essential to our lives, they also became more automated in direct proportion to their ability to be programmed and to be able to accurately measure their surroundings. Over the century, human decision-making was slowly stripped away as a combined human and machine effort toward the goal was made more efficient. At some point the wheel started turning more easily, and we call that power steering. At some point gears started changing themselves as needed, and we got automatic transmissions. Cruise control maintains a speed. Today, those so-called self-driving cars are, if not yet practical, at least en route and possible.

"Perhaps the steps toward automation in both biology and engineering and software are the same in some principle no matter the 'system' at play. I've been thinking about my economic hypothesis earlier, and it seems to hold. We could, for example, tell a story about the trajectory of the ecosystem of financial transactions in the twentieth century by comparing the kind and amount of work required for the same transaction between two people one hundred years apart. In 1900 many transactions were pen and paper via manual ledger and depended on a kind of social trust that carried the weight of the financial services and banking industry. Checks were hand-stamped and hand-signed for authenticity, and the expertise of a banker's human perception was one of the only barriers to fraud. Loans were based on identity and social trust, which is a fallible system based on stereotypes, intuition, and status quo. These days, there is automated fraud detection, automatic credit scores, high-frequency trading, AI-assisted mortgage and investment decisions, and huge amounts of machine vision and natural language processing behind the scenes in order to automatically read and understand checks, handwriting, and speech.

"But that evolution was not instant. It took decades. Do you guys know about the 'PlanPower' or its successor, the 'Client Profiling System'? These were early computers that spat out boutique financial plans for those earning over a certain amount of annual income for, of course, a six-figure license fee. In other words, to Blueprint's point, what was once done with guesswork and individual experience could be done suddenly and instantly by computers. It is unfair to say that the machines came for our jobs. They came because *we needed them* to fill in our perceptual weaknesses in a field with ever-increasing amounts of data. Finance simply has too much data for any one person or team to process. Today, only a few decades later, banks have algorithms behind the scenes for investment, debt, retirement, college, savings, insurance, budget, and tax-planning purposes. They can audit or execute transactions at the heart of the stock market in a few milliseconds or about as fast as it takes a neuron in the brain to fire."

Game Play: "Sometimes, automation can come just for the annoying bits." He looked over at Relentless for confirmation. "The entire success of Relentless and my company is in some sense part of this story. Everyone who had even stepped foot in a city knew that paying a taxicab driver with a credit card was disastrous. First, you handed them your card, and then they took a carbon copy of it with a swiper or sometimes ran it through a machine or maybe in a dodgy part of town they just stared you down silently until you backed out of the taxi without your entire wallet. Then the receipt if you were lucky enough to get one took about as long to print out as it took for the tree to grow to become the paper for the receipt. Then, you had to *sign* the darn receipt and do the math of the ten to twenty percent tip in your head all while you *had already arrived* and while still locked in the taxi because of all the people before you who ran out on their bill. It was maddening. *Everyone* hated the experience. And so, I worked with rideshare companies to create a frictionless experience where you hailed a car, and then as soon as you arrived at your destination you simply got out of the car and walked away. Everything was automatic. The pay, tip, receipt, signature, credit validation, money transfer between accounts, fraud avoidance, and subscription models. The transaction disappeared like magic, and customers were stunned at the grace of the experience. But it wasn't magic. The transaction had achieved what we call level four, or 'mind off,' automation."

Model Builder: "Exactly. The histories of both of these two ecosystems, automobiles and finance, are defined by a *similar trajectory* of automation. First, we start by doing everything manually and using our bias riddled and attebyte-weary, tired and stressed-out human brains. Then, over time, certain tasks become either so annoying or simply so overwhelming that we automate those. Next, lots and lots of data of the right kind is collected and fed into a programmable algorithm that makes the data actionable. Last, any inefficiencies or inconveniences are automated away so that the system autonomously improves continually, finding ever more powerful insights on its own. It happened with the car. It happened with how we transact finance. And it will one day happen with the body. We should write this down. Scribe, are you writing this down?"

"Indeed," I said.

Blueprint: "By now, perhaps some of you may see where I'm going with all this. I think about the automation over time in energy per unit of time terms. It's efficiency. It's metabolism. It's global biological efficiency. If the number of automated activities roughly doubles per decade, then we are due for a *metabolic* revolution in the way we behave, think, and triage our lives. The amount of literal energy we take in per day, which we of course convert to action and thought, is a fundamental constraint to what we can do or become in life. A single charge of your mobile phone gets you twelve hours of usage. Same is true with our thoughts. Our physical actions. To overcome or make optimal use of this limit, we use technology to expand and extend our abilities. There are extraordinarily simple examples like the wheel, language, the bicycle, fire, and so on.

"But if we want to think really big about the future of our intelligent existence, we are going to need more advanced ways of managing our biological energy expenditure. Achieving peak performance in even mundane or everyday activities can yield continuous improvements across our cognitive existence all while freeing up more energy to explore new frontiers. Think just about sleep, which is the biggest variable and determiner of a single day's cognitive capacity. Think about the trade-offs and how you currently make decisions surrounding your sleep environment and hygiene. Back to Scribe's morbid hand example, maybe we could ask: What would you give up for a good night's sleep? Conversely, what would you give up to *avoid* having a bad night's sleep? Up until very recently, answering this kind of question in a way that clearly ranks the costs and benefits of sacrifice relative to cognitive reward has been out of reach, which has forced us to rely on guesswork. The lack of data on associated costs about sleep debt or the effect of a poor night's sleep on cognition has resulted in our cultural norms devaluing and deprioritizing sleep. Less sleep does not get more done. It just shrinks the value of what's happening.

"Often, just like in many of these other historical examples, we find ourselves resorting to qualitative words or phrases. How we feel. How we look. We say we are 'tired' or feel 'foggy' or 'sluggish' when we sleep poorly. The closest we have to a quantitative approach is the number of hours we slept, which is, what, a subtraction problem, at best? Really? *That's the best we have*? We don't know how to give units to our sleep?

"Last year, I started acquiring data on myself with a combination of brain scans and wearables that gave pretty compelling evidence that a key aspect of my impulse control is strongly determined by the amount of deep and total sleep the night before. I had never had the numbers before. And then, one day, voilà, I did. When I surrendered to a more proper sleep schedule, I had taken the baby steps into, as you would call it, Model Builder, 'Level 0' of an autonomous system. I had started listening to the sensors and warning beeps and alarms and adjusted my behavior accordingly.

"This is the goal. The goal of any autonomous system is the demotion of the biased, frail human mind for solving problems within the system that the human mind is inefficient at solving. This is a key distinction to understanding the morality and social acceptance of any autonomous technology. What we want at the highest level of goal alignment is the ability to spend our finite, precious time and energy to explore the frontiers of being human. When we stopped having to wash clothes by hand in the nearby river, it freed us up for everything else society is now based on. One automation stacks upon another allowing us to focus on an ever-increasing list of higher-order endeavors. That's the whole point of all of this around us. Houses. Roads. Supply chains. We are slowly making more efficient things we once did slowly, by hand. When we know what all the liabilities are and when the goals are properly defined and aligned, we welcome automation. But when we *don't* know what is at issue, we treat ignorance as a threat. The social, technological, and economic world we live in can be an infinitely complex and an attention-grabbing place. We are bombarded with information, and our mere ape brains are often woefully unprepared for the tasks and severity of the issues. What will happen when we free up more attention, emotion, calm, and balance to focus on the right tasks? What will happen if we cement up our cognitive blind spots with level one or two systems?"

Model Builder: "It's hard to imagine what our minds would do with a new abundance of energy, but we do have two precedents in the billions of years across the span of life on earth: mitochondria, the 'powerhouse' of the cell, and fire. Billions of years ago, single cells had to do all the work—find food, run away, convert the food to energy, and all that. It was arduous work. Then, one day, a different cell, also weary and haggard, came along and proposed what was effectively a metabolic business arrangement: If you give me room and board, I'll automate the extraction of energy from food for you. Deal? Deal. With this newfound efficiency boost, multicellular life, and thus all life as we know it, was freed to bloom. Multicellular life is, effectively, a level two automated system. Or consider the harnessing of fire, which freed our *H. sapiens* ancestors from certain caloric and dietary restrictions and opened up energy, which was then converted to metabolism, time, and thought, for the little things to develop like, oh, *all of technology and society as we know it*."

Blueprint: "Exactly. I believe that a world of autonomous selves will open up a proportional step change in freed-up energy, which will then allow the upleveling of the modern human mind to whatever we will one day be. The change will be as powerful as the one from ancient to modern human. One can only dare imagine what we will do and what our experience of existence may be. We will have the opportunity to develop new industries, discover original uses of the mind, make iterations of governance and economics, and explore the thorny goal-alignment problems within ourselves, between each other."

The room was in what appeared to be a kind of stunned, hypnotic silence.

"This is why I brought Blueprint along, everybody," I said. "As you can see, he's a forward thinker. The writer Frederik Pohl once said, 'A good science fiction story should be able to predict not the automobile but the traffic jam.' The claim that everything in the future will be programmable is an *automobile* idea. It's not too hard to see or say that. It requires not too much imagination. Even Cognitive Bias could probably do it. But these alignment issues are *traffic jams.* So that's it. That's our dilemma. *How do we avoid the traffic jams?*"

Cognitive Bias: "Maybe ... we could start with lunch traffic jams? I'm hungry."

"Of course," I said. "I wouldn't be a good host if I didn't prepare you all your favorites. Blueprint, I didn't prep for you because I assumed ..."

Blueprint: "Yeah, I've already eaten my calories for the day. I would love it if you had sixty milligrams of caffeine somewhere, though? Today I can tell is a one hundred-twenty-milligram-caffeine day."

Dark Humor: "What now? Why? Trying to keep up with us geniuses? I'm honored."

Blueprint: "I wouldn't be. Let's just say ... it helps with certain metabolic processes."

Dark Humor: "Oh, this guy's a hoot. I bet your smoothies are all made up of blended versions of your future selves."

Blueprint: "I like the idea, but well, you know, *prions* are a thing."

Dark Humor: "You hear what you want to hear, buddy."

PART II: AFTERNOON

"The future is already here—it's just unevenly distributed."

—William Gibson

"Civilization advances by extending the number of important operations which we can perform without thinking about them."

—A.N. Whitehead

7: The Demotion of the Conscious Mind

Q: What sacrifices are worth it?
Q: How far is too far?

The plan was to let Blueprint run lunch from behind the scenes. Unfortunately, he didn't quite have the social capital yet to wrangle a group, and even worse, he seemed disinterested. Perhaps he had given up on fitting in. True, he was still a curio, someone the rest of the group seemed to dismiss as a fad dietician or maybe just a cleanse guru, and of course it wasn't lost on anyone here that Blueprint lived in the heart of Los Angeles, the very city that sued the US Supreme Court to undo a national ban on fortune-telling. The very city that has at its heart psychics, woo-woo, body modification, antiaging, pretending to act and acting to pretend, and Gold's Gym; a city with more monthly subscriptions to inject botulinum toxin into every unmentionable organ in danger of sagging than there are people.

I called everyone to order and sat myself at the end of a large table as people started to mill about, clearly getting hungry. The scene reminded me of experiments on monkeys where the scientists make them thirsty first to motivate them to do any of the oddball experiments for the sake of a sugary juicy reward.

This lunch could turn into a kind of experiment.

I just had to make everyone thirsty first.

"Of course, in the other room is a normal buffet full of great food for anyone who wishes to stress eat," I said. To nobody's surprise, Cognitive Bias immediately started heading straight to the other room. "*But...,*" I emphasized, stopping Cognitive Bias in his tracks, "...I also thought we might take a day and see what Blueprint is up to for lunch, and maybe, just maybe, anyone who wants could try that? It won't kill you. Really, it won't. Right, Blueprint? Actually, it might even do *the opposite.*"

Model Builder: "Our bodies turn anything we eat into the proper food it needs. You can lose weight eating whatever you want as long as you count calories and take a vitamin pill. We all know that."

Blueprint, quietly: "It's not just about calories." As all the others stood with their plates and started subconsciously stamping their feet on the ground like hungry domestic wolves, waiting for a signal to eat, Blueprint sat down calmly at a chair and pulled out a tin with a liquid, greenish goo inside.

The food looked like a slurry of seaweed chewed up and spat out by a dying bird. As Blueprint opened the tin, Dark Humor came over to peer over his shoulder. Dark Humor bent and proceeded to take a few exaggerated sniffs with the body posture of a proper wine snob.

Dark Humor: "It looks like that stage right between when a caterpillar turns into a butterfly. It's goo. It's all just goo."

Blueprint: "It's 'premasticated,' is the technical term. Blended."

Dark Humor dipped a finger in. Tasted it. Paused: "It tastes like prion strew. Unsalted *prion du jour*, please, waiter?" Dark Humor slapped Blueprint on the back with what appeared to be a kind of jovial, brotherly love. But Blueprint recoiled from the touch, as if struck by an unfamiliar hand.

Dark Humor: "I'll sit this one out, though. You guys enjoy your kuru. What's the buffet in the other room? I hope it's street tacos. Is it street tacos?"

"It is, in fact, street tacos," I said. "But your conscious mind can choose to have street tacos any day of any week, correct? Why not indulge me with the difference on this fine, final day we have together? If so, the appetizer is already on the table. For those brave enough to try the Blueprint protocol, we are starting with some of the purest, virgin olive oil one can get in the world mixed with little nibs of sugar-free cacao."

Model Builder: "Is this a joke?"

Blueprint: "It is not. If you eat all of it—the nutty pudding, the super veggie, the olive oil, and dark chocolate—just as I do, at the exact time I do, it's exactly 2,250 calories spread out over optimal times during the day to increase autophagy, reduce inflammation, and to induce all kinds of anti-inflammatory mechanisms. The perfect amount of high-octane fuel. Probably it'll do you all wonders, too. We don't have to listen to folk mythologies about what does and doesn't work. Many people could likely get away with doing this, all in moderation, and see orders of magnitude gains in quality of life without dialing it up to eleven like I do. The benefit *is* the customization. Nobody's individual health gets lost in population averages. It's also vegan, if you can handle that. Pounds of vegetables and nuts and oils, all designed to be anti-inflammatory. It's not the only way, of course."

Everyone was speechless. It might as well have been the sixteenth century and Blueprint was Galileo trying to convince the room that the Earth revolved around the Sun. A lot more still needed to be done to persuade them.

Farm Boy: "And you brought your own food? You just bring your own everywhere you go? That's quite sustainable, actually. If you look at food miles …"

Dark Humor: "Nobody even knows what food miles are, kid." He said it as a punctuation mark, not a question. Dark Humor had disappeared but had come running back into the room with his hands full. It looked like Dark Humor had snuck into Blueprint's room and grabbed some of Blueprint's things.

Dark Humor: "Look at this shit." He placed on the table the small metallic pill jars, the blue-light blocking goggles, the HRV monitors, olive oil jars, the bag of cacao, and the NuSalt. He just poured it out for all to see.

Blueprint paused, silently, to internalize how angry or annoyed he was going to be at the privacy intrusion and at the attempt to mock him in front of the group. Who would like having their nutrition cabinet spilled out in front of people? But the perpetrator was Dark Humor, and the outcome of his actions, though unintentional, would lead others in the room to understand the true severity of Blueprint's protocols, that he wasn't kidding, and that this wasn't just a fad. His calm reaction would be noticed as well as a possible benefit to the lifestyle. If he did nothing, he calculated, he came out on top. Besides, Blueprint didn't know Dark Humor too well, but Dark Humor's reputation preceded him before today, and everyone in the room knew to forgive him a few blunders. He meant well. He just wanted attention. For Blueprint to show that he was aggrieved at this moment would be to let Dark Humor win. I could see it all happen within milliseconds in Blueprint's brain. Not today, Dark Humor. Not today.

Blueprint: "You got me. That's all it takes. That and the twenty-six supplements I took this morning and the seventeen I'll take right now, after dinner, and the few others I take when I can."

Dark Humor: "After ... *dinner?*"

Blueprint: "Oh yes. This is dinner. It's two p.m., right? It's actually a bit late for me. But, you know, *travel*. Pain in the ass."

With a few quick gestures, I herded everyone's attebytes back toward me and the task at hand. I could feel with the silence in the room that everyone's mind had gone to simulating what life would be like if they lived like Blueprint. How boring it would be. Where pizza and weddings and dessert and dating and wining and dining and mistakes fit into the program.

I knew this was the moment. Strike when they're juice deprived: "All right, everybody, let's do it. I had a chef make some of Blueprint's … lunch? Dinner? We'll have dinner later, promise. Whatever Cognitive Bias wants to order. But please indulge me for lunch? One last favor," I said, with an impish smile. It had to work. I was dying, after all.

Dark Humor: "Fine, fine. You get your Make-A-Wish."

Just then Cognitive Bias slunk back through the doorway, a plate full of delicious street tacos in his hand. We all knew we wanted to be him deep down. Why couldn't bad things be good for us? The perpetual dilemma.

"Everyone, sit, please" I said. "Get your plates, and serve yourselves some Blueprint-approved slurry, buffet style. Remember to get to 1,977 calories. No more. No less."

Like prisoners, each shuffled toward their slop until, finally, everyone sat down and stared bleakly at their food. Cognitive Bias was already wiping his greased chin from the pork juice. He had gone for a second helping of nutty pudding and super veggie after having his fill of the street tacos.

I swear I could hear everyone's stomachs groan in unison with envy.

Self Critical, staring at his plate: "I feel like the color has been drained from life."

Dark Humor: "This is like that movie *Pleasantville*. The trailer made it seem like a comedy. Like right now how I *want* to be laughing. But of course, *Pleasantville* was an existential horror movie. Also, like right now."

Devil May Care and Relentless seemed to both be having a moment. Apart but together, if that makes sense. Their body language gave away that they were thinking approximately the same thing.

"What's on your mind, Devil May Care?" I asked, carefully.

Devil May Care: "Yeah, there's a bit of a paradox in my mind. I generally live life fully, right? Relentless, you might share this a bit. We move forward. Always forward. We don't seek dopamine or reward. I personally don't really even distinguish between rewards or sins. Or between what's good for me and what's bad for me. Things just are. As long as I survive. As long as I put one foot in front of the other. And the paradox I'm realizing right now is that usually that means I just eat not because it gives me pleasure but to achieve the cessation of hunger. Hunger just gets in the way. Colors the world like a false illusion. Switches the most dynamic form of intelligence in the known universe into a simple calorie-finding machine.

"Think about it. What if truly there is only just us out there? No other life forms in the entirety of the goddamn universe. Just … us. Which makes consciousness all the more precious and special given its uniqueness and the finiteness of its nature. It's just here. Just on this one tiny little pale blue dot. And despite our brains having the capacity to generate every known possible state of conscious experience or existence, it turns itself inside out and into a heat-seeking missile for calories when it gets a little bit hungry. Seems a bit odd, doesn't it? And so here I am realizing that if I don't need instant dopamine or reward or joy because really, I just care about the big picture

97

and damn the present, then I guess I'm actually confused why I *wouldn't* want or love this Blueprint idea. I mean, with it, I don't have to think about food, right? Which aligns for me. I don't *want* to ever think about food. If I could just turn it off and passively absorb calories through my environment, I'd do that trade in a heartbeat."

Model Builder: "Well, you wouldn't *have* a heartbeat if you chose that. Don't monkey's-paw yourself out of existence with such poorly defined wishes. Yes, some creatures in biology passively absorb nutrients, but these are all, you will notice, the most basic life forms on the planet. Nothing complex or complicated can do that. Mammals need to hunt or forage and eat almost all day, every day, just to keep the lights on. This is the price we pay for our extreme mammalian intelligence. We have to eat *constantly,* and we have to breathe *constantly* to break apart air molecules like little fission and fusion reactors into something we can use to keep our bodies buffered against environmental temperatures. The very price you pay for consciousness is your need to constantly stoke the fire, so to speak. There is no one without the other. That feeling of hunger you decry is the very essence of consciousness. It was probably the first sensation. The first conscious experience was probably being hungry, and we haven't turned back since."

Farm Boy: "Every animal I care for back at the farm, their entire existence revolves around food: when they eat, when they last ate, when they will eat next, and at what time and what kind of bleating sound to make if I don't feed them in time.

Ninety-nine percent of their—what did you call them, Scribe, 'attebytes'?—well, all those are dedicated to food."

Game Play: "But we are not stuck thinking what evolution demands we consider. We can choose what rewards us. Our attebytes are ours to use however we wish."

Self Critical: "It's not *this* that rewards us, that's for sure." Despite that, he was shoveling the nutty pudding regularly.

Blueprint noticed: "Surely, Self Critical, it is rewarding you on some level, or else, you would put the spoon down, no?"

Model Builder, interrupting: "Well, right now, he's conforming to social norms of the room, of Scribe's drama, and of the in-group cohesion in the room. These all give him a reward greater than the tacos—right, Cognitive Bias?"

Cognitive Bias, with a large smile: "You can have both."

Self Harm: "I agree." He stood up and went to the other room and came back with a plate of delicious tacos.

"Okay, let's pause and go back a moment," I said. "Earlier, Devil May Care, you mentioned that you just want to turn off hunger. So, what if we go around the table now and instead of grace or any of those guru, religious rituals, let's do a Blueprint version of grace. A thought experiment. Would each of you give over your free will to an algorithm optimized to give you your best physical and mental health? If an algorithm told you exactly what to eat when, and you were promised that you would never feel hungry again *and* that it would be anti-aging, anti-inflammatory, and let you live naturally and healthily as long as possible, would you do it?"

Relentless, with an exasperated and dramatic half guffaw: "Do I even need to ask? Even with your caveat, how do we agree on what 'best' means? Food is not the spice of life. How is the algorithm going to define the best way *for me* to live before it knows or even in the event that I don't know? I get joy from doing things with people, not with food, but since time immemorial we use food to gather people round. Yes, I like dinner parties, but it's not because of the food *per se*. It's the people. It's the camaraderie. Can I still have all of that if you remove the food from the food-based rituals? Something wouldn't quite be the same. We are hard-wired mammals to get our greatest joys sitting around a campfire eating with our wolves guarding us behind. Every dinner party or shared meal since, including this one, they are all just variations of that. I wouldn't trade that for anything. And besides, isn't your premise that my conscious mind doesn't know how to answer? Which is of course a bit of a Catch 22 to ask us to answer it ... *consciously?*"

I sighed. Involuntarily. I couldn't help it. "Yes, yes, of course. That ol' *super original* chestnut," I fired back, with an obvious and sarcastic tone. This was expected. All of it. People's answers are as common as dirt and about as varied as dirt, too.

I continued: "As a possible way of indirectly answering you, Relentless, consider the same answers given by those who answered the philosopher Robert Nozick's 'The Experience Machine' thought experiment. The idea of that is that you're sitting in a nice, comfy chair, and there is a fancy neurosurgeon behind you with your brain open, and the surgeon says they can implant a device and turn it on and give you the best subjective life imaginable, full of the illusion of wondrous accomplishment or anything your mind desires. *Anything.* The best life possible. Many people try their hardest to torpedo these contemplations and respond with trite clichés like, 'Oh, but sometimes I find myself learning valuable lessons from suffering,' or maybe they saw that *Twilight Zone* episode where the degenerate gambler thought he was in Heaven because all the slots kept winning before he slowly realized he was, in fact, in Hell. Because it was the thrill of losing and the ability to excuse his preexisting character and moral failures under the guise of a gambling problem that was the true benefit to his behavior. The actual victory or reward meant little. His brain's dopamine circuits were playing to *maximize* uncertainty, *not* to minimize it.

"So of course some aspects of 'optimal' will include pain or suffering or hardship. We all know that's how this works. We all know that's how life works. And so, for the sake of the contemplation, let's assume that, yes, all that is factored into account for the experiment. The algorithm truly optimizes for one measure and sometimes takes you through the valley of the shadow of doubt. For any part of the question where you worry about definitions, maybe just define it individually as some measure of the best performance or bodily health you most desire. Just so we can move on and not waste everyone's time. You choose the end state. The question should remain. The answers should remain."

Relentless didn't give in that easily: "Well, is this just for diet? Not for all parts of life? So the question *actually* is: Would I give up all choices with respect to diet, nutrition, and ingestion of all substances if I knew, or had some strong belief in, the promise that the outcome is ideal?"

Seeks Authority jumped in: "Actually, go back to your first question, Relentless. I like it. It's an interesting question, isn't it? How much of a life can be given over? We give a lot of ourselves over to our machines already. We trust them to give us directions rather than know how to get around town. We trust family and experts and friends and information sources. Those are mostly driven algorithmically now. So we are already parsing the world algorithmically. We receive information algorithmically. We decide how to get from point A to point B algorithmically because our smartphones just tell us to go left or right. But I sometimes get the feeling that my maps application is making me the control condition, making me go down the street and out of my way just so *it* can get better maps of under-mapped neighborhoods. Does that factor in? That in order for the AI—or whatever system you're imagining, Scribe— to have full control in an adapting, ever-changing world, it might have to do experiments. It might have to sacrifice individual health briefly to do the experiments, right? Is that okay? Would it tell us? We follow various governmental organizations guidelines about calories and recommended daily allowances and all kinds of health tips and advice without really even thinking about it."

"Good points, Seeks Authority," I said. "To answer you, yes, for now let's just keep it to diet, yes. But you raise good questions about the preexisting nature of the demotion of our conscious minds. We do it quite a bit already. We can get back to that. For now, first, let's just answer about diet."

Farm Boy: "Back in my small town, there's a saying all the doctors use. That the best and only way to get people to truly change their relationships with food and drugs and stuff is to alert them they are pregnant or have diabetes. Nothing else works. Ever. You can say they have lung cancer and ask them to stop smoking cigarettes like they tried with my grandpa. People don't stop. You can ask them to stop using drugs. Show direct proof that it's destroying themselves, their body, their mind, and their family. Doesn't work. They can have stomach cancer or intestinal troubles, and they won't stop drinking alcohol or coffee. Nothing works. Well-meaning, otherwise intelligent can be told to stop or they will die, and yet still, we see knowledgeable people engage in self-harm behavior every second of every day, all around us. So to me the question is a bit of a thinker. I tend to have to care for the diet and nutrition of all the animals on my farm because they either don't have the knowledge or ability to understand or care for themselves. So in a sense, *am I just their algorithm?* Because I know better? Because I have control? Who am I really to say? I tell them when to eat and what to eat. How different is it?"

Game Play: "We need to acknowledge the, how shall we say, non-edible elephant in the room. We are all speaking from a position of abundance and not scarcity. It is an immense luxury to choose *not* to eat those delicious tacos going cold in the other room simply because we wish to live longer. It's funny. Deny yourself the very nectar of sustaining life—*literal* calories—in order to live longer? Why? Because of a few studies in monkeys showing that they lived longer with fewer calories? Maybe they were miserable the whole time. Yeah, sure they lived longer, but to what end? Where's the units for joy? Contentment? Meaning? Purpose? The body is not a calculator. Life is not just the pursuit of quantified records."

Blueprint: "Of course, we are in fact speaking from a position of scarcity," came his calm, measured response. "Do you know anyone who has lived forever? *Age* is the scarce resource. *Time* is the currency. There are many kinds of inequality in life. Most *H. sapiens* born in the history of humanity, a little over one hundred billion of us if we're counting every soul that has ever lived, didn't live to be even twenty years old. Think about that. *Most did not even live to be twenty years old.* We are, in fact, talking about privilege and scarcity, yes, but your units are ... misleading ... at best. We are talking about life units, the scarcest and most valuable currency that has ever existed."

Seeks Authority: "But we also have a scarcity of autonomy. Of choice. An even scarier statistic, Blueprint, would be asking how few people in that long history of humanity *have had full choice over their behaviors*. I bet it's a whole lot fewer people than those who lived to age twenty. The most valuable and scarce resource in this history of humanity is not life units. It's not dollars. It's choice. The freedom to choose. Arguably, though there are still many, many people who live in abject poverty in their bodily and cognitive degrees of freedom, we are perhaps richer in total freely made choices, globally, than we have ever seen in the history of our species. Why take that away now that we have it?"

Model Builder: "It's not that simple. It's not just a one-way trend. Think about just speeding infractions. Driving. In the last decade or so, there's been a huge backlash against red light cameras in cities all across the United States. Of course, the cameras *worked*. But that's just it. They worked too well. Automated ticketing gave people the wrong feeling. There was always that small, human thrill of running a light or pulling a U-turn and looking over your shoulder for a cop hiding in the bushes and knowing they didn't see you and you got away with it. But when it's automated, joy and fairness, and, most importantly, *context* get lost. The rules of our society are not rigid, immutable, or passed down from on high. *They are contextual*. And so are our bodies. And so are our goals and desires. If you automate that away, you lose ... well, you lose *everything*."

Cognitive Bias: "Maybe I'm the wrong person to ask." He had the room in his hands. Nobody knew quite what he was going to say.

Dark Humor: "Oh, this should be good."

Self Critical: "Well, you'll get at least two votes in any poll we take—one per dinner."

Cognitive Bias merely grinned, as if he had been training for this moment his whole life: "How are you all defining what it means to be healthy? Virtuous? Let's take what we're assuming to be good things: to be in Gold's-Gym shape or have record low cholesterol or age yourself backward until you're a zygote again. Live forever! Be healthy! Do twenty pull-ups! Be attractive and healthy and happy, right? But *why* is that the virtue? We know there are societies where excess and indulgence were marks of wealth. Some of those people lived to be one hundred. They had it all, right? How sure are you that the AI won't decide, reasonably, that 'actually, according to our estimates, you're goddamn healthy and will likely survive multiple heart attacks and stents until the time medicine advances enough in the coming few decades to give you a replacement mechanical or clone heart whenever you need it. And you sleep well enough so you can lose a few hours of deep sleep, no big deal. And you won the genetic lottery with dementia—no plaques, ever. So you're good. And since we know all that, let's optimize you like late-stage Orson Welles. All the food and wine you can possibly eat.' What if it gets there on its own?"

Model Builder: "You know, actually, what Cognitive Bias is saying might be more than just a moral argument. In fact, modern AI systems have a very difficult time behaving and do all kinds of weird things when there's no obvious difference between two outcomes. We see this in almost every AI-trained system—if there's a state where no outcome is the optimal one with respect to whatever's being measured, they choose randomly. And it can appear from the outside to be very bizarre and sometimes even antisocial behavior. This doesn't really matter if playing a board or video game, but it would very much matter in terms of one's diet and health. So I sort of see what you're saying, Cognitive Bias, if I hear you right. You're saying, 'Well, what if the AI is good enough, and medicine is good enough, that total Orson Welles–level indulgence is actually what it suggests?"

Cognitive Bias: "Exactly."

Game Plan: "Look, it's important here to realize, I think, that we're not talking here about bannock and seal steaks. You guys all know Shackleton's adventures trying to navigate the South Pole? On his ship, the *Endurance*, they got stuck in the ice for two years, and they had to eat like bears about to hibernate for the winter when they were lucky enough to even have food. Their tonnage of supplies ran out, and they ate seal, penguin, and I think, even dog. Anything they could find. Did you know that about grizzly bears, that before they hibernate, they eat only the brains and eyes of the salmon? Throw away the rest of the body. How's *that* for a honed, quantified algorithm, Scribe? It feels like we already have a Farm Boy telling us what to eat and tending to our flock. It's called the HPA axis. Hypothalamic-pituitary-adrenal axis. It regulates our needs, desires, etc. How different is that from the force guiding the hibernating bear to change its eating patterns? Or having some omniscient AI tell you when or what to eat? Some part of the bears' inner decision-making process switches to desiring only to eat the very nutrients that will help them survive a future winter that hasn't even happened yet. How this happens is its own miracle. But clearly, they are playing a kind of game with contextual rules for survival. It's a different game than the rest of the animal kingdom in those few moments because, effectively, they are hitting the pause button on life and metabolism."

Farm Boy: "If it's anything like the wintry toads I know back home, they're just slowing down the record player. Not pausing. They still live even when hibernating. They still age, right?"

"They still sleep, too, I think," I added. "This isn't a loss of autonomy in the classic sense, though. They are still choosing to make the decisions to eat the brains and eyes only for nutrient purposes. That's no different really than being thirsty or craving a particular food. They are not controlled or stripped of autonomy. They are just ... shaped. They simply stop liking the rest of the salmon. They don't know why, though."

Relentless: "But this is getting dangerously deterministic. There are thousands of ways to argue that not even the conscious mind has 'will' if it's just being shaped by the body's needs and desires. I would much rather cede my willpower over to live a fully rich, adventure-filled life than a nutritious one. Who cares about food really? Nobody is over here saying how amazing Earth is because it's so full of the right kind of variety of calories. Sure, life on this planet and our very existence is incredible. It's *incredible*. And it's incredible in proportion to how much control we keep in the face of an environment trying to shape and control us at every turn. It's incredible because of us and our minds, not in spite of."

Self Critical: "What good is that control if it's all solved? Adventure is *done*. Over. We've explored everything, and that's what the conscious mind was best at for a while. Yes,

Shackleton. The South Pole. Check. The Moon. Check. It's all done. The era of exploration is behind us. We've mapped every nook and cranny of this planet. It's like what John Adams once wrote about generational progress and what we owe our kids. I love the quote so much I wrote it down in my wallet. Here it is, let me read it to you all: 'I must study politics and war, that our sons may have liberty to study mathematics and philosophy. Our sons ought to study mathematics and philosophy, geography, natural history and naval architecture, navigation, commerce, and agriculture to give their children a right to study painting, poetry, music, architecture, statuary, tapestry, and porcelain.' See my point? The explorers before us came and went so that we may build upon their progress. We don't need to keep exploring and adventuring. We can make art, instead. We *get to make art*. It's more than a right, it's a duty."

I took a poll. Asked if people thought adventure truly was dead. Every other person in the room voted that adventure was dead—the only abstention was, I should have guessed it, Blueprint.

But then a surprise.

Farm Boy: "Actually, I change my vote."

Farm Boy, no less.

8: Autonomy and Its Discontents

Q: Is life worth living without suffering?
Q: What is the next frontier to explore?

Self Critical, it seemed, was having none of the vote: "So you're all saying that we should be grateful to eat some caterpillar slop now because people in severe survival conditions one hundred years ago got by just fine on fried penguin legs, and now we need to, what, paint our inner turmoil because we *ought to*?"

Dark Humor: "Caloric restriction doesn't work when you're eating seal and penguin steaks. Not to mention the frostbite weight loss."

Blueprint: "I mean ... it, in fact, does work. As long as you keep minimal to optimal nutrition, of course."

Game Play: "The physical world is *explored*. Almost every inch of it. There's some stuff under water, and maybe someone will truly venture to the center of the Earth someday, or maybe

Mars or that one pure water moon of Jupiter but, c'mon, there's no such thing as Lewis and Clark anymore."

Blueprint: "There very much is. It's just no longer geography we explore."

Relentless felt his time was now: "Look, as someone who has climbed every mountain I can find, I do kind of agree here with Game Play. The world is done. Adventure is done. Nobody buys travelogs anymore because films and planes can take us there. Adventurers used to be celebrities. Marco Polo. Amerigo Vespucci. Neil Armstrong. Ernest Shackleton. They had royal or often nation-state sanctions. It was in everyone's economic, social, and human interest to just keep going. Keep expanding. Keep knowing. But we know what the Earth is made of now. We know its contours. We know space is too large to surprise us again anytime soon. What else is left? Scribe, not to be crude, but imagine tomorrow you are at the Pearly Gates or whatever the real equivalent is in the afterlife, and Ernest Shackleton is standing on the other side, asking what we know about the world that we didn't know before. Asking you what you did in your life to learn more. What did you do that was *hard*?"

Blueprint: "Why does adventure have to be a physical journey?"

Seeks Authority: "That's the definition." He looked around the room. "Isn't it?"

Blueprint: "I see no reason why the contours of a coastline are any more interesting than the shape a protein takes when it folds. Are you telling me we know the exact shape of every possible protein? Show me that map. Are you telling me that we understand where 'mind' comes from? Show me that map. Are you telling me that we understand biology and metabolism and how an immune system behaves sometimes like a liquid and sometimes like an ant colony and somehow all those millions of cells work in concert to protect their owner? Show me the battle plans. Do we have a map of the origins of our universe? Just tell me something, anyone here. Why are our genomes the size that they are? Anybody? Do we really know *anything* about the world around us? Sure, we know where to take steps and where not to. So what? That's not adventuring. That's map-making. Don't conflate the two."

Model Builder expected to be able to answer with some kind of rejoinder: "But humans have *been* everywhere," was all he could muster. He started to say more but stopped, disappointed in his ability to rapidly come up with an answer.

Blueprint: "Humanity has barely scratched the surface of what is possible."

Model Builder: "Okay, we've mapped the 3D world. That's something?"

Blueprint: "Is it? But who cares? Migrating birds understood much of the world's size and its contours long, long before we ever even thought to ask. They've seen magnetic fields and UV lines and soared between volcano peaks under their own powers. No human has ever done that. We've seen everything the world has to offer through our eyes and our eyes alone, but in no way whatsoever is that the only way to see things."

I recognized this tack of Blueprint. I threw him a softball: "You sound like Edwin Abbot."

Blueprint only smiled.

Seeks Authority: "The *Flatland* guy?"

"Yes," I explained. "From the land of the two-dimensional—Flatland, in the story—any three-dimensional object appearing in Flatland appears as a strange, indecipherable, cause-and-effect-breaking mystery of fleeting lines, shapes, and colors. It loses its depth and shape."

Farm Boy: "So? I don't really get why that matters if our world is in 3D?"

I said, "Well, we experience the world in 3D, but there are more possible, conceivable dimensions than just three. So, hypothetically, there is more to explain in the expanse of dimensionality on all sides."

Relentless: "Oh, come on. Are we seriously talking about, what, 4D Everest? Come on, that's a discussion fit for the side of a kid's novelty toy box she got out of a carnival vending machine. Or one of those prank puzzles. Not for serious contemplations."

Blueprint: "You are wrong, Scribe, about the lesson to take from *Flatland*." The room was silent. This was good. People were starting to come around to at least *listening* to Blueprint flesh out his ideas if not yet quite coming around to them. "This is not a lesson drawn from physics or string theory or time as the fourth dimension or anything remedial like that. This is about reframing the concept of spacetime to include what happens in the conscious mind. Think about the following. How do you each see, say, the mind of a prelinguistic cave man?

Seriously. Each of you. What do you think a mind of someone like that was missing relative to ours?"

Cognitive Bias: "It seems like it would be harder to learn lessons from long ago. When I chastise myself for doing something I wasn't meant to, say, it's usually in the voice of my mother or father or a teacher from childhood. But without language, what would those lessons look like? Maybe they wouldn't exist."

Model Builder: "Building off of that, I would go even more general. I would guess that the whole system of morality might not have existed before language. For exactly or at least similar reasons to what Cognitive Bias just mentioned—how would the social code get written if not in language or gesture?"

I had to interrupt here.

"Just as an aside," I said, "and I don't mean to interrupt—well, I guess I do, or else I *wouldn't have*, what a silly phrase—there are all kinds of examples in nature of social contracts without language per se as we know it. Vampire bats when they return from a nightly hunt will share their foraged blood meals with the children of other bats communally. But if you artificially inflate their cheeks with air so it *looks like* the bats have blood and aren't sharing, other bats will stop sharing their real blood meals with the social violator's kids. So, even without language, there's a social code that governs what is and isn't proper behavior in groups. All I'm saying is it's possible. Not that it has to be. Just that it might be."

Relentless: "It seems like it would be hard to have goals beyond the immediate. They would be like Nietzsche's dumb cows, just thinking about the moment. Just thinking about the present. And if I restricted myself to just thinking about the present, I cannot conceive of, say, ambition. There's no reason to climb Everest for its own sake. There's no reason to engage in these ambitious global adventures if you can't really define them outside just the banal existence of the present. Right? Ambition requires the future. And language makes the future. Without one, you don't have either."

Game Play: "This is interesting. I'm thinking that language was a key to what we think of as consciousness, perhaps. It allows for a generalized abstraction of objects to be sort of contained as the abstract category or grouping of that object. What I mean is, we've all seen the trees outside this house, right, and in the yard? Well, technically each is its own thing. There is nothing really 'grouping' them except our words for grouping them. And then our brains make up a category we call 'tree' and can say things like, 'We should plant more trees.' That wouldn't be possible without the generalizations and abstractions that language gives us. So, likely, nothing that we think would resemble 'thoughts' are happening in their heads."

Dark Humor: "We already know the answer. Feels a bit like interacting with Farm Boy."

Farm Boy: "It's interesting because what you just tried to do there, Dark Humor ... that wouldn't have been possible without language, right? Bullying. Insulting. If we were in a cave in prelinguistic Ice Age, you'd have had to throw a rock at me or come over and punch me or some other kind of dominance display to achieve the same effect. Instead you could do so at a safe distance using language alone. This is a kind of lesson about all tools, isn't it? The same tool can be used for good or bad. Electricity can power homes and be fashioned into an electric chair. Fire can cook or engulf a stake in Salem. Language can be used to expand minds or to bully. Or this dagger I have here, which can be used to skin a rabbit or, say, remove someone's tongue when it goes too far."

The message was not lost on Dark Humor, who slunk back against the wall.

"All right, boys," I said. "That's plenty. Self Critical, care to answer?"

Self Critical: "Well, maybe we wouldn't have had to abandon Depression like we all did." Silence in the room. He continued: "I mean, most of what got on our nerves about Depression was that he wouldn't shut up, right? It felt like he was inside all our heads just saying the same dark humorless shit over and over. At least I can lighten up when the situation demands it. At least, Dark Humor, we can all just ignore or bowl over with the lightest comeback. And, Devil May Care, who will probably kill us all one day, at least we can predict what he's going to do next. Always the dangerous thing. But Depression was like a linguistic savant. The poet laureate of purgatory confining each of us in his chains with words alone. We all felt it at times, and we all hated his words at times, even if we accepted it some of the time. So maybe, just maybe, there wouldn't be depression, and we wouldn't have ever known Depression. Almost seems worth it?"

Blueprint: "It would not be worth it. And I know you don't really believe that. Humans are terrible at counterfactual reasoning like this. To truly remove language from our minds we have no real way to consider what consequences this would have on our cognition. It would likely be devastating in ways we can't even imagine. But the fun part is taking these contemplations and applying them to *what's next* for cognition. Just imagine this. Just imagine that five hundred years from now people look back on *us* the same way we do on those Ice Age hominids who couldn't speak. What if we, one day, will be as far behind cognitively, relatively, as cavemen are to us? Is there any reason to believe at all we have reached the peak of human consciousness and ability? The burden of proof is in many ways on those thinking we have somehow hit a ceiling than it is on anyone claiming we haven't. What if one day we could actually walk a mile in someone else's mind? What if we could feel what it is like to be the ocean, the forest, and the bees? What if we could live history instead of reading it? What if we could conceive of four- and twenty-dimensional shapes? What if we could, instead of destroying our enemies, destroy the *concept* of enemies? What if we could be more kind, empathetic, and compassionate? What if we could communicate telepathically with a new language that is 100 times richer in conveying thought, emotion, and experience? What if we could internally channel the genius of a writer, scientist, or artist? What if we could eliminate cognitive biases, compulsive behavior, and destructive tendencies?

"Are you sure, *sure*, that we are not just at the very beginning of an explosion of human consciousness and cognitive capability? Are you willing to stake the entirety of the human race and the survival of our species on that claim? What if the only way out of the Cognitive Paleolithic is to strive to uplevel ourselves out of the modern mind which is, by the way, also frail, ambitious, bullying, timid, and riddled with bias and error?

"*This* you all call the end of adventure? I posit that adventure need not restrict itself to the 3D world of rocks and dirt and coastlines. I posit that there is an infinity of exploration still to be done and that such exploration will happen inward. We must venture in. Not out to the Poles. Not up to the Moon. In. *In.* The next unexplored frontier. How many possible species are there? Only a fraction of one percent of them still survive to this day. The permutation space of biology is larger than the configurations of atoms in the known universe. We can and will and *must* explore as much of this parameter space as possible. We need to know what it is like to combine brains. To halve them. To know what it is like on the other side of the cognitive wall that limits us to all of our territorial, pedestrian, present-minded errands. You are all just floating around in life like it's one long flight delay. And the first step to adventuring is to unlock the organs in our bodies so that we can unlock the mind's actual, full potential. Not in the life coach way. I'm just talking literally, metabolically, about freeing the mind from many of its pedestrian notions by automating away the stuff we don't need so that the mind is freer for other harder concerns that it is better able to handle.

"Think about when single cells combined and made themselves into a partnership. One cell became the mitochondria, said, 'I'll handle the metabolism stuff, you take care of the rest,' and then the outside cell, its partner, its symbiote, its colony, was free to do more. Who wins in this trade? The outside cell that must border and battle the ravages of the world or the mitochondria, which gets to happily set up shop and still, three billion years later, is alive. Arguably, the mitochondria is the most successful living organism the planet has ever seen. Why? Because we are its shepherds and not the other way around. It has remained mostly unchanged for billions of years as life and Earth devolved into a mess of different species and messy and failed evolutionary experiments. All the while, the mitochondria sat peacefully inside *all* of our cells. It bet with the market. If any life survives, it survives.

"And so, when you say adventuring is over, I say: 'It has just begun.' Why? Because we are still struggling with the outside. Because we are shackled and bogged down by all the manual tasks required to live day-to-day. We are still trying to do everything. Instead, we should hand everything over to automation and our AI symbiotes so we may sit back and let our minds take care of what they are best at."

Self Critical: "Nice speech, but how can you know there is something over the horizon? Something on the other side of the Cognitive Paleolithic, as you call it? It seems to me that all the primary evidence we have argues that we are pretty much as good as we're going to get. Sure, maybe one day we'll sleep better, and nutrition will stave off some dementia so that the total number of attebytes dedicated to cognitive, rather than earthly, concerns will increase proportionally, but ... so what? Isn't that just asking for more hardship as we fracture into more haves and have-nots?"

Cognitive Bias had finished his lunch, made an espresso, and was rocking on his feet, clearly agitated, and trying to get a word in.

"Cognitive Bias, care to say what's on your mind?" I asked. It was my last day. I could playact as moderator as long as people seemed to listen and respond.

Cognitive Bias: "I think I'm hearing these arguments correctly. It's difficult for humans to imagine the power of new emerging technology, right? If we were with Gutenberg in 1,450 and we said, 'Imagine the ideas that will be written about using this printing press,' we wouldn't be able to do that much with the prompt. We certainly wouldn't be able to imagine today. Or when electricity was discovered, did people truly imagine *all* that it would power? That we'd have a tiny Voyager spacecraft at the edge of our solar system stealing the Sun's photons to power itself alchemically with electricity? That would be madness to have predicted. Absolute madness. Or when the Internet was created to send large files between universities, could anyone really imagine the Arab Spring or that the world's elections, celebrities, and wealth would mostly one day exist on the Internet? Our imagination ends at the beginning of the unknown."

"Beautifully put," I said.

Cognitive Bias: "So I'm a bit unclear, Blueprint, as to what you're saying. There seems to be an inconsistency. On the one hand, you're saying that we are at the very beginning of the new road toward a kind of upleveled conscious experience that we can't even imagine. And then, on the other hand, to get there, you're saying that we need to demote the conscious mind as much as possible in the right contexts. That the default cognitive mind is often trying to trick us. That is our nemesis. So which is it? Is it the enemy, or are we merely at the beginning? Because the 'demotion' you speak of does not sound like you wish to advance the conscious mind. It sounds instead like you could not domesticate it yourself and couldn't control your own, so you are foisting that failure on all the rest of us."

Dark Humor: "Damn, you've grown up, CB."

Cognitive Bias: "Scribe made me rethink some things."

Blueprint: "Say more, CB. I can tell you're not done." He used Dark Humor's filial nickname for him, which was a clear sign of respect from Blueprint. Everyone picked up on it. We were getting places. And Blueprint was right: CB wasn't done, but he needed more time than some of the others in the room to think up what he wanted to say. It was Relentless and Model Builder who had no problems saying what was on their mind at any time to anyone. Others in the room had a more measured, nuanced way of approaching things.

Cognitive Bias: "I do, I do." He was feeling the group's approval and thriving on it. "I think I would just offer the opposite solution while agreeing that the problem is the same, Blueprint. We *do* need to increase our cognition. But I think we need a *promotion* of the conscious mind and not a demotion. It is already our friend and valuable symbiotic partner. It is what enables everything we value. It gives value to value itself! How could you possibly want to demote the very rare and special thing that makes us *us*? I suppose I'm a bit of a Luddite in that direction, then, if Blueprint's goal is to merge more and more with technology, I say we move more toward Farm Boy's approach."

Farm Boy: "Hey, careful. I'm not a Luddite. I use tractors and drones, pesticides, and some fancy nitrogen-fixing bacteria that eliminates a lot of past mistakes from the soil. Game Play hooked me up with it a while ago. One of his Silicon Valley things. I don't claim to understand it. But it works. I just appreciate the land and working with my hands as well. There's a difference."

Cognitive Bias: "Nonetheless, what I mean is that perhaps we should train and hone our conscious mind to be better at its weaknesses rather than simply ignoring them. To get around obliquely to your question over lunch, Scribe, why give yourself over to algorithms? Why not train and shape one's conscious mind to be better able to fix its own flaws and work toward proper decision-making without the need for fixed external constraints on choice? This isn't just 'Have your cake and eat it, too' logic. I mean that we can have our cake and *choose* not to eat it. There's no paradox. There's no demotion. We keep intact all that we thrive on and from—ourselves, our brains, our will, and our discipline—and we use it to give all the benefits of which you spoke, Blueprint. I see no reason why we can't promote the conscious mind. Perhaps it needs *more* control. Maybe once we give it the tools to listen in on all the body's organ systems and its needs, maybe it can make the right choices. It just needs the data. We don't need to give it to the panacea AI you are imagining, Blueprint. We already have all the tools in here, in our heads."

Blueprint: "Tell me, CB, have you considered that your conscious mind is behind such thoughts?"

Cognitive Bias: "Behind?"

"Propagating. Creating. Spreading."

"Well, of course I'm conscious now so, sure, I guess? What does that tell us?"

"Have you considered that like any form of life, or stage of life, that has ever existed, it might have defense mechanisms?"

"Sure, I'll allow it."

"And have you considered that your vociferous defense of the conscious mind is, in fact, the first layer of its defense mechanism?"

"I don't see how that could be."

"No, of course you don't, because it's hard to imagine contemplations on what the other side of the Paleolithic looks like. The modern mind is fine. I get its value. Its usefulness. It got us here, after all. It got us to the Moon. It gave us language and math and computers and chemistry labs that can piece together almost anything nature can. We are approaching nature's powers in scope and ability, which is terrifying but also awe-inspiring. We have in front of us the chance to perhaps even *do more* than nature ever could with just the tools she's

124

given us. I am not saying that I am certain that there are better horizons the further we go down this path of automation and coevolution with our most intelligent tools. What I *am* saying is that the world still has unknowns. Still has a gray fog of war covering most of conscious existence. Still has Here Be Dragons sections of the map.

"And the most important realization is that when confronting this fact, there are still two types of people. The explorers and those who stay home. There are people to whom the existence of such a fog will give deep anxiety. And there are people who stay home. When Shackleton put out an advertisement seeking volunteers for the *Endurance* trip to the South Pole, there were too many volunteers to even interview. Some women even dressed like men at the chance. And some who saw the exact same advertisement did nothing except become ever more sure that they wished to eke out an existence in early 1900s Ireland and Britain just like all the others before them, then and hence. Some choose to take the clarion's call, and some ignore it by digging their heels in even more deeply into the stability of the land they treasure under their feet. This isn't a new phenomenon we are experiencing here in this room right now. This is simply a tale as old as time: some see a sunset and get mad at not knowing where the Sun goes at night and follow it to either their death or a brief resolution of their anxieties, and some just stop to enjoy the moment, go home, and sleep peacefully. I hope that you sleep peacefully at night, CB, I really do. But I do not. I do not trust my conscious mind for certain tasks.

"It was neither evolved, made, nor honed for many of the modern Herculean burdens we put it through. It fatigues easily. It is a victim to the whims of temporary lacks. It cannot imagine what it cannot experience. It deprioritizes information that flies in the face of its prior beliefs. It is irrational, irreverent, and lies all the time. We are stuck with all the cognitive quirks of all our ancestors before us who lived in very different environments. Our bodies and minds are riddled with a hodgepodge of genes from viruses and bacteria that we stole and randomly shoved into our genomes somewhere. Imagine doing that with software or with code. Imagine having a data center that powers the most important computations on the planet and it just randomly has bits and pieces of computer virus code sprinkled in its source code. That's what a human mind is. Flawed and error-prone because it wasn't made or designed; it was cobbled."

Model Builder: "None of that matters." The mood in the room was moving against Blueprint. Perhaps he had gone too far. "And it is absolutely the case that a modern data center was built off the back of decades of computation and engineering lessons learned by millions of circuits trying their best to do what they need to do. No modern data center is made weaker from its history battling software or incompatibility or com-puter viruses. Except for those that die, which is what happens in evolution too, by the way; one is left with a messy patchwork, yes, but inside that messy patchwork is *robust-ness*."

Game Play: "This. Yes. That. I agree with Model Builder. Much of the messiness you speak of, Blueprint, is not a lack of cleanliness or function, it's a defense against the randomness of the world. I've told you all by now about the 'robot in the sand' analogy, I'm sure, but it seems to fit perfectly here."

Blueprint: "I don't know it."

Game Play: "It's exactly what Model Builder is saying, in a way. The conscious mind is messy *because* the world is messy. None of the cognitive biases are irrational outside the context in which they work. It's not the conscious mind that needs tinkering but the ways and kinds of contexts we put a mind *in* that need careful consideration. Our flaws are not flaws. Our biases are not just that. *They are tools of adaptability.* Think how insane the modern world is. We sit with glass boxes in our rooms and can beam almost every single surviving song, picture, or film into this glass box *in an instant.* And what do we do with that? We use it to look at what other people are doing to feel bad about ourselves. That's *insane.* So why do we do it? Because our brains used to spend time and metabolism to check in on others in our social tribe because that was *extremely useful information* at one point and because there was a limit to how much information could be gleaned in an afternoon in the African savannah. Pre language, it was just eye contact and body language and who is fighting whom, and who is fucking whom, and who is throwing dirt in each other's eyes. That was it. That's what social media was back in our primate days: just looking where other people are looking. And so our brains evolve to value that extremely useful information, but now, with the tiny glass box in our pockets that contains a live copy of all the world's information in it, our brains go haywire.

The finite resource of social currency is not infinite, and we can't help ourselves. In other words, what was *once* not a bias or quirk of the brain now is but only in the wrong context. It's not the brain that's the problem. It's the world it gets put in.

"Now think about when a brain really breaks, like with paranoia—or a brain with a conspiracy or conspiratorial mindset, which is just a form of paranoia, really—each of which are one of the worst tricks a mind can play on itself. But they are rational in narrow confines. The FBI *does* have files on some people. People *are* lying sometimes to effect their own ends. These are all events that have nonzero chances of being true and that have happened and will happen again. The truth value of even the wildest conspiracy theory is not what matters. What matters is that inside the conscious mind of whoever believes these wacky ideas is an internally consistent and rational model of the world but one that just has the wrong premises about likelihood of the probability of interacting or individual events. A conspiracy brain is not riddled with irrationality. It's simply making the wrong conclusions from the same evidence we all have. But they aren't irrational. They are, mostly, just *unlikely*.

"Likewise, many of what you are calling the brain's flaws or quirks, Blueprint, are actually rational in the right circumstance. They are not *wrong* universally. They, as improper thoughts, are just mistakenly taking priority at times when their premises are unlikely. The timing is what's wrong, not the belief."

Dark Humor: "So Depression *was* saying true things? Just at the wrong time?"

Seeks Authority: "You can't really believe that, can you, Game Play?"

Game Play thought for a minute as the room stayed silent. Calmly, slowly, he responded.

Game Play: "There are statements for which no context is appropriate, correct."

Blueprint: "But both your points remain, Game Play and CB, and they are good ones. And if I may take a step back here, I think my point has been made. CB, while I do in fact believe the conscious mind should be demoted, I am not wed to the idea. The goal is the goal. The data is the data. My intention was simply to bring up the unresolved nature of the limits to consciousness, cognition, and our default mind not to offer a solution to any but simply to make the bigger offer: That more need be discovered. That we are not finished. That there is more adventuring to do. And that I am, like Shackleton, putting the advert up on the wooden telegram pole, offering a port and a boat so we may float together in the cognitive seas and weather her dangers. The very existence of debate, I believe, proves my point: We may not all be adventurers. But adventure is not dead. Which means that 'explorer' is still perhaps, and more than ever, the most important role in modern society. Why? Precisely because most have given up. Precisely because the most ambitious thing people can imagine anymore is going to the *next* cold rock in the sky instead of focusing here, back at home, at the limitless borders of the inner world."

9: The Sirens' Song

Q: What do we owe our past selves?
Q: Can you fire your evening self?

Relentless looked over at Seeks Authority to see what he would say first but took the reins instead.

Relentless: "I, personally, can say that I find it useful to demote my conscious mind *some of the time.* That's the important part. Sometimes you just simply give yourself over to a higher cause or pursuit or, in some cases, a deity or something. We all live *for* something. It can be family. It can be the *idea* of family. Or philanthropy. Activism. These are all kinds of calls to arms. These are all causes. And if you are using some third-party guide as a heuristic to your life, to the rituals involved in eating or socializing or what is and isn't a sin or what is or isn't taboo in one's life, is that not so different than demoting the conscious mind already? We do it *all the time.*"

Seeks Authority: "It's true, what he's saying. The very nature of our body's metabolic and cognitive processing is that we can trust it, that we should trust it, that we need to trust it at times. When we need oxygen, sensors in our blood tell the brain that too much CO_2 has accumulated in the blood, and so we hyperventilate. When we need water, sensors in our organs tell us to feel thirsty. When we're hungry, horny, tired, you name it— these are all us giving in to a natural algorithm that evolution made for us, gave us, and never asked whether we wanted. And we know it's an algorithm because it can be turned off in special cases. Those afflicted with rabies are afraid of water no matter how thirsty they get. This is, on its face, absurd. The conscious mind should obviously be demoted in certain extreme cases like that. Why not in all cases?"

Devil May Care: "You wish to *reverse* evolution? It gave us a mind for a reason!" He was, oddly, an originalist when it came to the body. He would shovel energy drinks and stay up all night, but he would never change the building blocks of the body or mind. He believed the body arrived naturally in its best shape and that whatever you chose to do with it was part of the agreement with nature. The body will robustly return to homeostasis as best it can, not just so long as he, its driver, was free to do what he wanted but precisely *so that* he was free to do what he wanted.

Devil May Care very much saw the body as his own property for his mind to do with as he pleased. Perhaps, I was starting to wonder, if that was the intellectual major wedge between those who disagreed with each other here now in the room. Perhaps if the conversation instead moved to property rights and the sense of ownership over one's own body, clearer lines in the debate would be drawn.

Blueprint, having finished his meal, seemed spry, lithe, and energized, like a boxer in a corner between rounds, ready to spring back into action: "Let's see where this comes from, this idea that the conscious mind should be in charge at all times. This seems a very natural and very inertial argument. That it is the way it *ought* to be because it *already is*. That we should keep the conscious mind in charge of all decisions because it already is. But it isn't. That would be absurd. On the most basic level we know that conscious awareness of stimuli is lagging behind the actual stimuli by a few dozen to a few hundred milliseconds, sometimes. That's just basic physics. That's how long it takes the signals to reach us.

And we further know that the brain is stitching things together, after the fact, all to make one's behaviors, wants, motivations, and thoughts appear to be both obvious and carefully considered. But are they? Are we sure the brain's reasons for accepting or denying something are the true reasons? If not, are we sure we want a liar in charge?"

Game Play: "Now, that's too far. No need to go that far. It's not lying. Lying would have the force of intentionality behind it, and I think we can all agree that there is no intention."

Blueprint: "Sure, for now let's say that it doesn't. It could, of course, be subject to Darwinian evolution by natural selection just like all other kinds of information in the universe, but yes, for now, let's say that it cannot have the intention to mislead."

Game Play: "Not only that, but it is also right *most of the time*. Yes, of course there are some illusions like a straw bending in water or maybe some people see things slightly differently in the world, but so what? All of our minds, with the exception of any psychotic or hallucinatory ideas, are getting it right most of the time. This table underneath all our plates is real, has been real this whole time, and our brains have been accurately and consciously perceiving its edges perfectly every second we've been in this house. Nobody has run into any walls. Nobody has run out screaming because they misperceived the lightly burned tortillas as a true raging inferno in the kitchen. The conscious mind has proven itself time and time again, over hundreds of thousands if not—if we believe some theories—hundreds of millions or billions of years, and it is effective, reliable, and useful. Where is all this hate coming from? Forgive the pun, but I do truly, deeply believe this is the wrong game to play with life."

Farm Boy: "I had this herding dog, once, as a kid. All it wanted to do was herd sheep or ducks back home at night. It would nip at your ankles anytime you tried to go off on a walk or ignore it, too. Cutest thing imaginable. And as it got older and older and its knees started getting arthritic, we figured it would enjoy retirement after a life well lived. And so we gave it the cozy, warm barn all to itself full of toys, food, and blankets. We would spend hours with it every day. We didn't realize it, but for the next few months, what we thought was placid contentment in his body language was actually grief and boredom. It didn't understand that it had done well or the idea of retirement. It didn't understand that we were happy with it and loved it and cared about its inner world and were trying to offer it peace and relaxation. All it knew was that it could hear the sheep outside, and they weren't being herded. Each bleating footstep was probably torture to the poor guy, trapped in his retirement jail. We got it wrong. Very wrong. And, Game Play, I wonder, are you worried too that the demotion of the conscious mind would ... put you to pasture, so to speak? Would be your retirement, with no more conscious games left to play? Maybe that's the heart of your concern, actually. That if everybody demoted their conscious mind, then everybody is playing the same game, which means, ultimately, that nobody is playing *any* game."

Game Play stayed silent. Thinking. Ruing.

Blueprint: "Can I ask you two,"—he gestured at Seeks Authority and Relentless, who had seemed to also form a physical pact in one corner of the room—"if you would fire the evening versions of yourselves? I am not speaking just idle words here. I am saying that, if so, you should entirely remove the ability for your evening self to make decisions."

Cognitive Bias: "Late evenings are, in fact, when I seem to have the least self-control. He's onto something."

Model Builder: "This is normal. This is sundowning. The brain uses up energy and collects debris, like any living system, throughout the day. When we are hungry or tired, our ability to control our own behaviors and gestures reduces. There was that classic study with Israeli parole judges, right, where they were more likely to *grant* parole, which was by far the harder and riskier decision, when they were well fed or rested after a break. Perhaps one could frame the argument in those terms if we imagine the conscious mind like the parole judges and say to ourselves, 'You only get to decide during optimal cognitive conditions,' and we know, *know for a fact*, that late at night when we are literally at the furthest point from the last bout of restorative sleep we had, that we are not capable of making the hard cognitive decisions then. In a way, you revoke its charter. It loses its vote at the board meeting. So to speak."

Seeks Authority: "I had to do something similar years ago, in fact. My doctor had mentioned one day when I got off the scale a 'wake-up call,' which, trust me, are some of the last words you want to hear from your doc. For ten years, Evening Seeks Authority had overeaten and gained more than fifty pounds, which kept up the cycle of fueling relentless shame, guilt, and malaise. Every night, Evening Me failed the marshmallow test and temporarily discounted the future in favor of the here, the now, the carbs, and the sugar. His behavior had devastating ripple effects on Morning Me. It ruined my sleep and caused Morning Me to be quite displeased because he consistently felt tired, irritable, and unprepared for the demands of life. In short, Evening Seeks Authority was making life miserable for *all versions of me.*"

Self Critical: "You don't live on an island either. Every night or trip with you had started to turn into something to regret after the fact or to dread beforehand. So many countless times we'd wake up on Kilimanjaro or in a cabin or even if we were just in a hotel, and you'd just be up the morning, chugging coffee, *not* going for a run, and bemoaning how few deep sleep hours you got the night before staring at your laser ring readout like it was a fortune cookie of past, present, and future. It got tough, to say the least."

Seeks Authority, with a pained look: "I could tell. That's why I changed. So, a few years ago, I fired Evening Me from his shift, revoking his authority to make food consumption decisions. Now, no matter the circumstance, only the a.m. parole judge version of me can decide when, what, and how much to eat. Honestly, the results have been spectacular. I lost sixty pounds and with less to carry around, I have fewer cravings, and I've never felt better. I'm well rested and sharp, ready to tackle the challenges of the day. CB, give it a shot."

Cognitive Bias: "Excuse me?" He was already snacking again.

"But you don't go as extreme as Blueprint, do you?" I asked.

Cognitive Bias: "I don't think so. What do you do, Blueprint?"

Blueprint: "Usually, I eat breakfast at seven a.m. and dinner somewhere between eleven and two. No caffeine or very little, and no other stimulants at all. I discontinue fluids after four p.m. to avoid getting up at night."

Dark Humor: "Discontinue fluids?"

Blueprint: "I stop drinking. I think you'd be amazed at what a truly healthy minimum of nutrients or input our bodies actually need. Our bodies still think the world is scary and lacking. We hoard because for most of life on this planet, hoarding was completely rational."

Self Critical: "It *is* for most people on the planet, still."

All in the room knew this was true. There was no getting around the fact that, again, they had found themselves discounting luxury. Those who had it defended its use or, in some opinions, misuse; those who didn't decried its lack.

I responded, "The same could be said, and was probably said, for every era and every time in the history of the human race, though. No explorer ever left at a time when the world was fertile and fed. Shackleton brought tons—literal tons—of canned food and supplies with them to the South Pole, and all the while back at home there were starving street urchins all up and down Ireland and Britain. His goal was bigger than the time he lived in. I see your point, Self Critical, I do. But what is one to do? There is unequal access to freedom and food and wealth and water all the world over. There has been since day one. Is that everybody's burden at all times, or do we just plod on, one foot in front of the other, each with our specialized skills to change only a small slice of things?"

Dark Humor: "Well there's the strongest point I can see, Relentless, against firing your evening self from dietary decisions." His tone was surprisingly humorless. "It makes the choice to starve look like just that: a choice. Voluntary. Perhaps that reduces the empathy felt for those who have no choice but to be on caloric restriction, who have no choice but to be vegetarian because they live on a farm in Uganda and can only get dairy or a monocropped island like Java and just eat rice. Or Ireland and their potatoes. You get the idea."

Blueprint: "The choice to not choose does not reduce empathy, Dark Humor. In fact, it makes it much clearer that the *conscious choice*—remember, one *chooses* at first to decide not to choose anymore—to subsume their conscious mind should increase empathy for those who have no choice but go through the same ordeal. The only way the sacrifice of firing one's evening self is manageable and palatable is to recognize that the choice was theirs and that they must live with it. This likely will increase empathy for those when it becomes apparent that they couldn't choose."

I asked, "Are you all familiar with the 'Ulysses contract' concept in mental health?"

Nays around the room. I had an idea. I said, "The basic idea is that Ulysses wanted to experience the Sirens' song, which on listening caused sailors to become mad and dash their heads against the rocks or drown in their pursuit of the song. And so he stuffed all his crew members' ears with wax so they couldn't hear it and he made them chain him to the mast of the boat so that he could listen to the song without fear of jumping in and drowning. He knew he would say anything to get them to release him, so he also made them promise not to untie him. And it worked. But what's that have to do with mental health, Blueprint?"

Softball.

Thrown.

Blueprint: "Ulysses demoted his conscious mind by giving it over to an algorithm." It felt in the room, if ideas were objects, like the gauntlet was finally thrown down. "The algorithm was simple and social—commands to his crew to not listen to him at a future time, no matter his plea. This is used sparingly, and controversially, in mental health care here in our country for those with episodic psychoses or any kind of phasic disorder of volition or control. Bipolar, schizophrenia, some forms of treatment-resistant depression, etc. The basic idea is that during a lucid phase, when they feel like they have their full faculties and their conscious minds are playing no tricks on them, they agree with their doctors or family on how they would like to be treated if they do happen to have an episode. Just like Ulysses. It works great for some. But there are legal and ethical and of course medical challenges to this. Who says who is in charge when? Can you really, almost like a living will, contractually bind yourself to demotion of one's future self and consent? Does medical consent fall off with some sort of half-life? Is it a currency and one either has it or doesn't? These are extremely thorny questions, and many doctors won't adhere to Ulysses contracts because they don't believe in their ethical, legal, or scientific validity.

"But for the sake of getting on to the afternoon, let's say that the legal challenges are out of the way and the only questions are moral. Is it moral for the individual to sign a Ulysses contract? Is it moral for the doctor and family to adhere to it? In Ulysses's case he had command of the ship, so there was less in the way of executing the plan. If he was kind, perhaps he would have let every sailor experience it, in turn. But no, he wanted the experience exclusively for himself. Take note of that detail, adventurers in the room. But I digress. Really the issue is about whether one's present self in any way has a duty, or any causal power, over a future version of one's self. If we break apart the selves, as you do, Relentless, into let's say two versions—let's call them Morning Self and Evening Self—and treat them as different moral entities for the time being, the question might have more to do with spheres of influence or dominion than what is or is not beneficial to the individual. Of course there are some artificial constraints. We cannot do the simple moral equivalencies like tie Evening Self to a train track and ask whether and in what circumstances Morning Self would pull the lever to divert the train because it would mean death to the both of them. But we *can* ask about moral causality between the two, I'd say. We *can* ask what right Evening Self has to control Morning Self and vice versa."

Game Play: "Exactly. *Exactly.* Why should I trust Morning Game Play any more than I trust Evening Game Play? If Evening Me wants to harm Morning Game Play, let it. All the abstentions from social and the joys of night life are Morning punishing Evening, are they not? So why is one self allowed to punish the other self and not vice versa?"

Blueprint: "Why is one version of Ulysses correct and the other restrained?"

"That's not the same."

"Oh, but it is. The analogy is that letting the conscious mind control dietary and health decisions in the evening is as dangerous as listening to the Siren song. It leads, inevitably, to an accelerated and rapid death. Or if you prefer, letting the conscious mind control dietary and health decisions in the evening is as dangerous as not being in control of one's full faculties, as in the case of an episodic mental break. In both cases, there was a more-in-control and more rational version that gets deferred to."

Game Play wasn't convinced: "No, it's not the same. There's a crucial difference because, arguably, both with Ulysses and with this manic-depressive person they are flipping between two states: able to give consent in the one case and not able to give consent in the other. But that's not the same thing. Evening Self is very much able to think, choose, contemplate, love, learn, laugh, all of it. Evening Self is a full person. To deny Evening Self agency is to deny the *very existence* of Evening Self. But if you respect me as a person, and if you respect future Morning Self as a person, who by the way also doesn't even exist yet, then you also have to respect Evening Self no matter their choices, don't you?"

Blueprint: "And so Ulysses, you'd untie him from the mast?"

Game Play: "No, of course not. But he's under a spell. His volition has been conquered. Been countermanded."

Blueprint: "Good, good. I agree. But how different is that than failing the marshmallow test or the parole judges who are more conservative the more tired they get? Have not their volitions been countermanded, as you say, by the present need for sugary reward or by a reduction in their cognitive capabilities? How can we say what it means to have full faculties at any given time? Is it not true, like what was said earlier, many times, that we behave as if there's a lack of certain resources out in the environment—say, sugar or social information—and so we overindulge in the modern world, which is replete with both? Shouldn't it be possible to say that in such cases, watching such behavior, their will has been countermanded? Imagine two scenarios … maybe this can be our twisted version of the trolley problem, in fact. We are standing on the boat with one life preserver, ready to toss it into the ocean for two of our fallen comrades. One, to starboard, Cognitive Bias has jumped over and is swimming toward a marshmallow sitting calmly atop a floating log. And two, to port, Ulysses has jumped over the bow because Game Play over here freed him under the guise that he's a true, real person at all time points, and so is swimming toward the Sirens. Who do we save?"

"Well, CB, of course," I said. No need to hypothetically kill off a friend on such a day as today. "Anyone else? Perhaps a vote. I vote CB."

Relentless: "CB."

Model Builder: "CB."

Seeks Authority: "CB, of course."

Farm Boy: "CB."

Devil May Care: "CB."

By now the tide had turned. It would be almost rude to save a mostly fictional and mostly dead character from a book almost nobody here had read.

Self Critical: "CB."

Game Play: "CB."

Dark Humor: "Frankly I'm shocked. Couldn't CB make it to the marshmallow and back just fine? It's not like he's dying from it, right? And just being contrary: I vote neither. They chose their risk as individuals. Might as well save the life preserver for someone who values their life, you know?"

142

Blueprint was unbowed by the plurality in the room: "I, and no offense, CB, agree with Dark Humor that the answer should be neither at first. But of course we should use the preserver. So, I say, flip a coin. Not because both are largely at fault or in charge of their decisions, but instead because, I believe, *neither is more or less* at fault. They are both victims of an algorithm they can't control. That algorithm is their conscious mind that is tricking them into thinking false beliefs about the world. In CB's case, that sugar is in high demand and, in Ulysses's case, well, we can't know what that's like, so I won't even try to describe it."

Devil May Care: "Sounds nice, though. I bet it's a really nice song. Like Adele, I bet. I kind of want to hear it. Is it on Spotify, does anyone know?"

Dark Humor: "No, you cannot simply stream the mythological song that lures gods to their deaths."

I said, "It feels like what we're actually talking about isn't what we think we're talking about." I wasn't entirely sure where I was going with this, but the room stayed quiet for me to let me think it through. "Let's take what we all agree on. That there are times in one's life when one has more or less control over their actions. Right? That's what is in common across the parole judge, Ulysses, marshmallow, and Evening Self examples. But this feels like the age-old scientific query: Are we talking about *kinds* of difference or *degrees* of difference? That's a big distinction. It seems, Blueprint, like you are saying that there are kinds—that is, categories—of difference. One is either in control, like Ulysses before the Sirens, fully or not at all, like when he's begging to be released to swim to them. And then a few of the rest of you seem to be saying, 'Okay, sure, there are differences, but they are only minor differences in degree,' and so, for example, Evening Self has maybe only ten percent of the willpower units that Daytime Self has, and we shouldn't hold that against him because really who the hell can know what the variation looks like throughout a day or what the margin of error is on that estimate."

Blueprint: "That's a fair point, Scribe. Crudely, however, and without agreeing on units, can we all agree that an Evening Self has less faculties than Morning Self?"

Farm Boy: "I just don't see how you know that. Sometimes when I'm out really late tending to something like a new calf or wolves or wild boars and maybe don't sleep well, I'm a zombie in the morning. I don't feel nearly myself until a hearty flapjack breakfast. I don't quite understand which version of me during which part of the day or night I'm supposed to trust most. I like all versions of Farm Boy."

"We do too," I said, warmly.

Blueprint: "Sure, sure."

I could tell that he could tell he hadn't quite convinced everyone yet. Maybe not even himself fully.

Blueprint: "I actually don't know, Scribe, that the dividing line between opinion in this room has to do with the perpetual clumper-versus-splitters dilemma or degrees-versus-kind dilemma in science. I think it's much simpler than that. I think it might have to do with the *amount of perceived harm* that Evening Self can do. And here I perhaps take a stronger stance than most in the room. I view Evening Self as a person as weak as Ulysses in the face of the Sirens' song and who is equally willing to sacrifice the health and vitality and even existence of body and mind for a few meaningless hedonistic pleasantries. And when you view it with this severity, the options are very clear. One must remove Evening Self from the equation. Yes, one is still in some way choosing this with one's conscious mind. The idea is not to demote the conscious mind as some 1984-esque, totalitarian blanket statement. The idea is simply to predict when we are less able to make clear and coherent decisions and enter into a kind of Ulysses contract with one's self where they cede the need to be tied to the mast at night."

Dark Humor: "Figuratively?"

We all knew the joke he was making.

Blueprint: "Call it what you will."

Dark Humor: "A 'dominatrix' is what I will call it."

"As I said, call it what you will."

"A 'dominatrix' is what I will call it."

"Are we in an infinite loop?"

"I don't know. Maybe you should ask her what you think."

I had to interrupt the fracas. "Okay, gentleman. Gentleman. Be gentle. Let's move on," I said.

What few had paid attention to except me was how everybody in the room, in their distraction, had finished lunch. In fact, more than a few took seconds and seemed to have totally forgotten about the food in the other room.

Relentless: "Are we really talking about just diet here? I have a sneaking suspicion you're talking about something much bigger here, Blueprint. That true?"

Blueprint: "In a sense, yes, I am. The phrase 'demotion of the conscious mind' is chosen as the kind of unofficial slogan for my endeavors, but I say that mostly because it's usually provocative enough to dislodge heavily entrenched norms. I do *mean* it, of course, in a narrowed sense. A more accurate way of stating it would be, perhaps, 'Elevate and defer your decision-making to the most capable physiological instances of self via an algorithm that is superior to your natural abilities.' We are better at sleeping at night, right, based on circulating hormones and their peaks? This is physiologically driven by our biology, genes, and by evolution. We have circadian rhythms for exercise and performance, right? This is also physiologically driven by our biology, genes, and by evolution. We have narrow fertility windows for trying to make a viable fetus. This, too, is physiologically driven by our biology, genes, and by evolution. See the pattern? I am simply saying that we likely also have physiologically driven peaks in our cognitive clarity and that we should pay attention to those moments and, perhaps, let them drive many of the larger decisions, which involve uncountable variables at timescales which we don't understand. I'm not saying I know everything or every peak or counter in my metabolism or cognition. What I *am* saying is that, much as our organs are specialized to carry out different tasks at different levels of efficiency and we trust them to do so, we should equally recognize that our brain's functioning and our ability to reason through hard choices and—no offense, CB—overcome the hundreds of cognitive biases that riddle us *also* has valleys, peaks, and troughs and that certain times of day are specialized to handle cognition better than others. Our brain is a biological entity and organ just like all the others. It responds to available energy and metabolism and all the vagaries of biology and life throughout any given day. What good does it do us to ignore that fact?

"We all feel more or less in control at various moments throughout the day. But the conscious mind doesn't really let you sit on that fact. Even if you cut the brain in half or give it a stroke that causes hemi-neglect and the person is slurring and mumbling and making no sense, *they will think they are making sense*. The greatest trick the brain ever pulled was convincing you it knows why you did anything ever. And since we know that it can turn on us at any moment like the Sirens' song, I ask each of you: Will you put wax in your ears? I promise that there is a more beautiful and richer life on the other side of that decision."

Devil May Care: "So we *do* get to listen to the song after all?"

Blueprint: "No. Unfortunately you have to come to terms with the idea that life itself is the reward. That is the song we pay for."

Just then, I heard a pronounced and resigned sigh but couldn't tell if it was just one person or all in the room, together, at once.

10: The End Is (Some Percentage) Nigh

Q: Will the world end?
Q: What should we do if the solution is dystopia?

As everyone finished their lunches ("dinners") it became clear the discussion wasn't just about the food or motivated by feigned fealty over a shared meal. To my surprise and delight everyone still milled around and not simply because they were unsure what to do next but because they were eager to keep going with the debate.

Clearly nobody thought it resolved.

Seeks Authority: "I have to say it ..." It seemed like he was asking himself for permission to speak, which felt like growth. "I have to. I'm worried, Blueprint, that even if I agree with you—even if you convince all of us in this room, today—that this isn't an idea that exists in isolation. This isn't just a 'You Won't Believe This One Diet Trick' idea. This is a much bigger and systemic idea about automation that generalizes into something much more far-reaching. The basic premise, as I hear it, is that the human mind isn't capable of or up to the task of reasoning or thinking through the most difficult problems that face us. If the conscious mind can't even be trusted not to binge on late-night snacks despite the harm to one's future self, it is not hard to imagine how we can say the same thing for the human species writ large: We are binging on fossil fuels and self-destructive behaviors and war to the detriment of our future selves. We always have. We always will. Is that the idea?"

Blueprint: "Precisely."

Seeks Authority: "Well, then, frankly, I worry about the potential for nation state, totalitarian, and technological abuse if this premise catches hold. It's a tale told many times over that technology goes first to the powerful and that the number one response to power by the powerful is to hold on to their power as if their life depended on it. And the classic way to do that, going all the way back to oh, I don't know, the primordial oceans, is to limit the degrees of freedom of any who stand in the way. This is single-celled warfare. This is global geopolitical warfare. It's always about more or less degrees of freedom though we sometimes speak about it in different terms. Maybe it's just a branding or PR issue, but it is getting increasingly hard for me to hear the 'demotion of the conscious mind' and not think of authoritarian regimes salivating at the idea. Denying people their choices. Denying people their rights. There's a certain utilitarian coldness to a human body creating a homeostatic or protected environment where cells must die when they age, and all foreigners are to be tagged and attacked by the immune system. If you scale this up to the entire world, aren't we talking about the mass repression of thought? Of mind? Isn't that *1984*? Isn't that *Brave New World*?"

Blueprint: "Right, right. What I hear you saying is, 'Okay, fine, maybe a nice algorithmic-inspired diet and health plan is acceptable for an individual to extend their life span or optimize their health, but the greater version of this, at a global scale, could be used for evil?'"

"Basically."

Devil May Care: "It's more than a PR problem. It's a basic methodological problem. There is no way to reduce people's freedoms and come out of it sounding like the good guy. Even with a single person. Especially with all of humanity. None at all."

Model Builder: "It's interesting the way you described that just now. Why is this proposed technology a reduction of freedoms whereas other technologies of efficiency and algorithms—take, as a simple example, mapping and direc-tions, which is entirely algorithmic and way more efficient these days all driven by the 'demotion of the conscious mind' because the conscious mind turns out *kept getting us lost* and can't possibly store every road in the world—aren't described in those same terms? Couldn't we just consider this sort of hypothetical, algorithmic life coach or AI or whatever it is to be like providing us with efficient routes for our cognition and behavior? It already does so for our steps and our cars when it routes us from point A to point B, right? Really, how different is it than mapping idea A to idea B or rerouting around cognitive traffic?"

Cognitive Bias: "And by 'cognitive traffic,' you mean ... what exactly?" He looked like he wanted to be offended but wasn't quite yet.

Model Builder: "I mean inefficiencies, quirks, biases, or fatigue. Any suboptimal decision-making routine. Why should-n't we reroute around it the same way we reroute around an accident or traffic on the roads? When someone is obsessing about something out of their control or says they are so hungry their mind can't stop thinking about food, isn't this cognitive traffic? And maybe sadness or attention deficit are like accidents or speed traps. Why should we reject assistance out of hand?"

I interrupted, "I didn't take that to be Seeks Authority's point. I think he was saying something much more about the historical sweep of things at scale. And I think he's onto something. There's a difference both in execution and moral outcome between doing something at an individual level and doing it on a societal level. A very difficult question is to ask what such technologies would have implemented were they to have come online sooner in human history. What if we had the power to give ourselves over to algorithms in the Dark Ages, during the Crusades, or during the worst years of slavery or colonialism? Would not the technology have been used to 'demote the conscious minds' of the subjugated given the pretense of efficiency, health, age, or whatever glossy shiny ideal was in vogue at the time?

"If so, it means we should think about the history here and recognize that history is not always fair to ideas or people.

Nietzsche, for example, had his works usurped and reused by his sister after his death—literally, edited and redone—to fit an ideology that would be widely abused in the twentieth century and justify untold evil acts. So, just to be blunt, let's take Seeks Authority's worry all the way to the darkest possible conclusion it could reach. Let's say, for example, Blueprint, that your ideas take off. Earth is in peril. Global warming is getting way, way worse. Humans don't seem to be able to solve anything, and you get put in charge and your mandate is to extend the life span of the human species using all the tools and knowledge you gained doing Blueprint-like things to your body and mind. What would you do? Just so I can start to envision what this looks like in the big picture. It would be helpful."

Blueprint stood up and started pacing. I figured I'd explain it to the room. Most, it seemed, had already gathered that.

"He thinks best when pacing," I said.

Blueprint: "Thank you for this question. First, I would do everything possible to get a readout of the health of the planet not in subjective terms but in grounded, scientific fact. What's the equivalent of a blood panel for the entire Earth? What's the equivalent of an EKG or a brain scan? Can we get those? A good model to think about would be the air quality sensors that are now distributed all over the globe but mostly in industrialized countries. They give a pretty good snapshot of a particular and highly dynamic measurement that changes on the order of minutes or hours. I'd expand that to cover some sort of sensing of the oceans and an even distribution of sensors all throughout the land and air and, sure, probably even space just in case there's a proxy correlate of global health only detectable from outside low Earth orbit. Why not, right? I'd have all the world's supercomputers dedicated to running simulations and essentially doing double-blind experiments on any and all possible-to-engineer variables including all the hidden ones no human has ever thought about. The most important thing is that this system would have no priors at all or first-principled thinking built into its assumptions. I respect all the geophysicists and scientists and all those working hard today, but we have to be realistic that they probably don't know *everything.* We simply don't know yet how *everything* works. And if the survival of our species is on the line, I'd try to combine all of that data and look for surprising variables. Look for *zeros*, as Game Play would put it. Once we know that we can effectively feed an unbiased and comprehensive snapshot of the planet's status, we can start to learn about the variables behind how to move it toward rather than away from a picture of its health."

Farm Boy: "Forgive me, but who chooses what 'health' means? I'm confused about that part. On my farm, we kill certain insects because our goal is crop yield. If the goal was, say, keeping the greatest number of locusts alive, then, well, we'd have to do something different. Human health is different from the health of every species and often it means a kind of extermination, hunt, or trapping ..."

Self Critical: "Amen. This is no different a conundrum than the earlier thought experiment about whether we would give ourselves over to live the quote best unquote version of our lives. Nobody really knows what 'best' means, and they especially don't while they aren't living it and can't even imagine it. At least Blueprint seems to be pretty honest that his goals are to live as long as possible. And the 'fountain of youth' thing is a clear and good goal because at the very least we *get* that goal. We understand it. We can define it. We know the success conditions because it either is working or it isn't. It either worked or it didn't, and it's been a goal of some people going back as far as history goes. Ironically, many have died in its pursuit. If you compare years of life taken to years of life added by the search for eternal life, it is one hundred percent weighted toward the life years *taken* side."

Cognitive Bias: "This doesn't have much to do with Seeks Authority's original question, does it?"

Seeks Authority: "It does, in fact. Right, Blueprint?"

Blueprint: "Deeply, yes. It does. People have performed unspeakable horrors under the guise of saving the world from imminent destruction. It's too easy a trope and too scary a story to ignore. Think about how many religions have an apocalypse in their past, present, or future. A second coming. A flood. A plague. A Holy War for their very survival. The big worry, even if I was in charge of designing a kind of Plan for humanity, would hinge on the moral equivalents required to act when the algorithm demands action based on the story that the world is in danger. Most of the time, throughout most of human history, that premise has been incorrect. An exaggeration at best. Even during some of the scariest few minutes of the Cold War, we weren't talking about a full and total extinction of our species. Just a very, very, horrifically unpleasant reset for the few lucky survivors. But *H. sapiens* was down to only a few hundred during the worst bottlenecks of the Ice Age. We've come back. And so one of the most important questions for this moral exercise is determining how we can say, with certainty, what the stakes are. I believe that the stakes are existential as much as I do that human life is finite and we all die sometime. Only if you truly believe the premise that our entire species is in peril do such drastic measures as the demotion of the conscious or some variant of it make sense. It is an extreme solution to an unprecedented problem."

Model Builder: "That's exactly the point. I see it now. I could easily imagine the algorithm ... Can we name it, by the way? Does anyone have a good name for the AI that oversees all the planet's health? Well, anyway, I could easily imagine the algorithm deciding to perform the equivalent of 'demoting the conscious mind,' which would mean ... oh, I don't know, getting rid of all the scientists or academics or politicians who have control or large-scale degrees of freedom. This would do it, right? That would be the equivalent to lobotomizing the human species. But that's also—and, Scribe, please correct me here if I'm wrong—what the Cultural Revolution was in China and Mao's purges and Stalin's purges. These are all attempting to cut the cultural head off the cultural snake, so to speak. Entire societies had their conscious minds demoted. So the question I wonder about is, what would it look like to implement some of the individual body's homeostatic drives on a population or even planetary level? We might not like what it takes."

"You are mostly correct about the historical purges," I said. "Except for the teleology. The end was not salvation but obliteration of dissent in those historical cases you mention."

Model Builder: "It *was the salvation* of a certain, particular way of thinking and ruling. It's all just a point of view, no? One of the more confusing and nuanced parts of this debate for me is the severity of the AI's possible solutions. Even in Marvel's comic book universe, one of the biggest of the big bad guys was a robot designed to protect the planet who decided, possibly *rationally*, once it had enough data, that the 'heroes' of the world and our lovely protagonists were actually more net harmful than helpful and so needed to be destroyed. Maybe that's always what an AI concludes when it has enough data about us. How do we know that the solution to saving us isn't just keeping a few of us alive like batteries, *Matrix* style, or killing us all, *Avengers* style?

"The fiction and mythologies that we create these days are in fact handling many of these same moral quandaries and technological questions about oversight and overreach. I was just watching a video on the lessons professional Go players are drawing from the new AI that can trounce any human, and the general gist is that the AI are extremely good at understanding and exploiting *sacrifice*. They throw pieces into the middle of the maelstrom of the enemy's position because at the end of the hundred-move battle they are ahead by a fraction of a point. It's ruthless and calculating and doesn't take into account the possibility that each of the pieces can suffer, has consciousness, or feels pain. We have human values that are more important than survival, I'd say. How do we quantify those?"

Blueprint: "These are extremely tough questions. But this idea of sacrifice is a bit of a scaleless phenomenon, isn't it? Just to keep going as living, breathing human creatures, we are sloughing off and turning over millions—billions—of cells in our lifetimes just to keep the engines running. Immune cells attack weakened cells that might become cancerous. Skin turns over constantly, probably also to reduce risk of mutation. And despite advances in synthetic food, we literally must eat other life and must eat other life *constantly* to keep ours going. Every plant and animal here is a sacrifice of some sort, all for the immutable and seemingly unquestioned moral correctness of just being alive. How different are these morals if the idea is just to ... keep living? There are trade-offs everywhere, all up and down the chain of life. There are sacrifices. There is death. All of that—all of it—would be useless if humanity goes away one day. It would all be for naught. So I do not wish to avoid the extremely difficult question on sacrifice. It is, in fact, central to the discussions we were having earlier. Would you cut off your hand to survive if it was stuck? What's the equivalent for the human species and entire planet? What would you sacrifice to live longer and healthier? Would you sacrifice coffee and alcohol and ribald Bacchanalian dinners with friends to do so? These are the same questions over and over again. Perhaps I misread the room. I thought we had all agreed that sacrifice was an endemic and natural part of progress?"

Cognitive Bias: "But sacrificing part of one's *own body* pales in comparison to what could be done that is sacrificing others' lives and perhaps their well-being for the sake of what amounts to a belief. Isn't this religion all over again? Faith-based doomsday criers shouting from the mountaintops?"

Blueprint: "Is it? I think perhaps you are simply under-estimating how quickly and how bad things could or will get. It's almost like Pascal's wager but for our very existence. Our planet either is or is not headed toward extinction of all life. You either think that's inevitable, imminent, or avoidable. By choosing not to act, you are making a wager that it is not imminent and perhaps not even inevitable. Inaction is still a bet here. I think if all of humanity—every piece of art and thought and moment of love and joy and family and happiness—if all of it was to be at stake, with humanity and its arm trapped under a rock, you would in fact sacrifice quite a few of the pieces to save the whole. Someone here brought up Shackleton. That was a journey of sacrifice, great and small. People lost toes. They missed out on many a warm dinner with friends. Why? *Because they couldn't not go.* To some people these are the easiest decisions in the world."

Game Play seemed agitated: "Can we return to Seeks Authority's point earlier about this being *Brave New World*-esque? Let's unpack what that book was about. In that world, automation has become so integral to society that Henry Ford himself is so revered that *time itself* resets to where the year the Model T is introduced becomes Year 0. Literally the creator of industrial-scale automation is revered as a god and supplants another mythology entirely. It is a world based on science and efficiency, and children are slotted into social classes because that's their designed role. It's all about large-scale, global efficiency. Pesky things like cognitive biases are eliminated entirely mostly by getting rid of all emotions and therefore much of thinking in children. No more pesky *emotions* to get in the way of *reason*! It's a fully technophobic, dystopian nightmare. But it's essentially a thought experiment about what would happen, Blueprint, if your ideas generalized fully, right? What if the algorithm tells us that the exact setup from *Brave New World* is the only path forward? Would you do it? Would we?"

Dark Humor: "Well, there's very good data on whether people follow their noses or their feet into dystopia. The surprise horror at the end of *1984* was that there were cameras behind the televisions. And now I don't even think you can buy a new television that *doesn't* have a camera. We have all volunteered for this. It turns out everybody underestimated the power of the human mind to care at all about the slow erosions of its freedoms."

Devil May Care: "And here we are, again, rehashing the same basic argument. What unique features of what we believe to be the essential human experience are we willing to give up? Do we give our hand if it's trapped? Do we deny ourselves food or company for the sake of cognitive cleanliness? Do we believe biases are sins and worth ridding the world of? Do we believe an apocalypse is coming of such epic proportions that drastic measures are needed?"

The room turned into a cacophony of voices as one added to another. I had trouble taking notes, so forgive me if the attributions here are incorrect or ambiguous. I did my best.

Dark Humor: "You know what was drastic? Building an Ark. But that worked out for him."

Relentless: "No, Dark Humor. Those are just stories. Stories. Stories. There wasn't ever a real flood. If you *had* built an ark and waited, you'd be a fool, not a visionary. What he should have done besides was try to *stop* the flood. There's a reason the film *Waterworld* flopped. Nobody wants to live like that."

Model Builder: "If we take a step back and realize what's in common across these conversations, it all becomes clear. Almost all of our differences hinge on whether one believes in the severity of the proposed possible outcome. Whether staying trapped under the rock will one hundred percent kill you in the end or whether you have X percent chance of being rescued. Whether the world is ending anytime soon or not is also probably different in each of our heads. My guess is that if we all had one hundred percent shared conviction about the severity and certainty of the default outcome, this would in turn set our moral guidelines to be similar. I think there's more similarity here than we realize."

Seeks Authority: "Look, I'm in if you guys are."

Farm Boy: "I'm confused—we're not actually deciding anything, right?"

I decided to interrupt.

I said, "Let's actually do that poll. It's a good one. Everybody gives their guess as to what percentage chance humanity has of destroying itself and our planet within, let's say, within two decades. Blueprint, you lead."

Blueprint: "One hundred percent."

Devil May Care: "Zero percent."

Self Critical: "Eighty percent."

Farm Boy: "Five percent."

Seeks Authority: "I think I started the day at fifty percent, but now I'm more ... sixty percent?"

Relentless: "Zero percent."

I said, "I'll go too. Ninety percent."

Cognitive Bias: "Zero percent. We haven't gone extinct yet, have we? So why would we? It makes no sense."

I said, "Just a number will do nicely. Game Play? Any guesses?"

Game Play: "Five percent. I think we can engineer any—"

"Just a number will do nicely, thanks. We can debate after. Zero, what do you say? Dark Humor, thoughts?"

Zero: "It would be weird for me to say anything but zero percent. So zero percent."

Dark Humor: "One hundred percent. Why do you think I say the things I do? Might as well while we have the chance. There is no posterity to be judged by."

Model Builder: "I'm with CB here, actually. Zero percent."

There was silence in the room as we realized how much time during the day had been, perhaps, spent in waste. What we had really needed to do all along was start with *this* question and divide the camps into those who imagine a bleak future versus those who don't and let the pieces fall where they may from there. There is no way the severe solutions proposed by Blueprint with respect to the body or the world could be agreed upon by people who don't even buy into the very premise that things are dire and in need of fixing. Who would have guessed that the very premise itself requires an imagination that not everybody shares? In a sense, I was glad we arrived here if only because things might have gone in circles ever longer had we never done so.

I said, "Well, that's interesting. I guess we should have started here."

Blueprint: "Not at all. It was the perfect time. The room divides nicely, and we can continue. On the doomsday side we have me, Scribe, Dark Humor, and Self Critical. In the middle, no surprise, we have Seeks Authority. And on the other side, we have Devil May Care, Zero, Relentless, CB, and Model Builder … you all say zero percent. Let's start there. Why? Why not? Care to unpack your optimism?"

Devil May Care: "I just have a deep feeling that is actually more of a belief, that things will be okay. Humanity has been through a lot. A lot a lot. We've had religious crusades and Ice Ages and constant war and volcanic explosions and the Cold War. We've faced innumerable pains and predators, and the whole world is basically trying to kill us. Seventy percent of the planet is a liquid that kills us in two minutes if we don't breathe. That's *insane*. We can't even look at the Sun without going blind. This is a harsh, hostile world, and yet, still humans try to climb every peak, dive every trench, and continue to be as ambitious, playful, and artistic as we can. It would be very easy to survey the world and give up. I don't think we will ever give up. The plight of the *Endurance* is exactly what gives me that hope. Even if all the world dies off and there's only a few hundred of us left, we will persevere. We will engineer a solution. The conscious mind can play tricks and get bored and sometimes get in our way, but it mostly gives us the ingenuity to wriggle out of *any* problems we may face. And if those problems are climate change or war or another asteroid or some Yellowstone super volcano going off or whatever, we will make it. We always have. We always will."

Relentless: "Amen. Couldn't have said it better myself. I even occasionally, and this is a dark thought, wish something like the apocalypse would happen. I personally think I would thrive. I'm used to putting everything on the line for the sake of an idea. And the story of the survival of humanity is the most powerful tale we've ever come up with. That's why religions and cults use it to such great effect and so often: *it works*. And personally, I haven't heard a single 'problem' with the planet that engineering can't fix. If we can cause it, we can *un*-cause it, or whatever the word would be."

Zero: "I have full faith that the principles behind Zeroism, the philosophy Game Play and I have been working on, will save us in the long run. Ultimately, the solutions we imagine for the future pale in comparison to the problems we can foresee because the problems—climate change, overpopulation, war—are first-principled extrapolations from our history and data whereas the cleverest of the *solutions* are necessarily impossible to see. They are zeros. They come at the tail end of zeroth-principled thinking. So there will always be a mismatch between a problem and its ultimate solution. That's why I'm not worried. Zeros will save us, and soon a new form of intelligence created by our AIs is going to be cranking out zeros left and right. Engineering zeros. Social zeros. Scientific zeros. We are on the very edge of a precipice that's going to be an explosion in knowledge and human capacity within the next generation. Within a few decades. It's here. The only problem we will ever have to worry about, truly, is alignment with our tools, our selves, and our planet. It's urgent, yes. But we do have time."

Cognitive Bias: "I agree with all of those. I just don't see how we could possibly blip out of existence. I think we're in the earliest of the earliest stages of human progress. We are still fetal as a species. This is the beginning. There will be trillions of humans one day, spread throughout the solar system. We have barely begun. I can't see any other path. Just look at the rate of progress and its recent explosion. Why would that stop?"

Model Builder: "I want to recant slightly. I actually would abstain. I'm willing to admit that I simply don't know enough about any of the underlying variables at play to even hazard a guess. For example, I don't really truly understand what it means for coral to die or the ocean to acidify. Part of me thinks, 'Okay, great, things will definitely change, but they *already* changed to get to where we are now.' What I mean is, sure, things will change. Deserts will become flood plains, and flood plains will become deserts. The north will de-ice. Greenland will turn into a global tourist attraction with a gorgeous pristine lake at its heart once all its ice melts. Canada will become the

165

richest country in the world when it controls the world's shipping. Equatorial diseases that many industrialized nations have no experience with will spread as their host ranges expand to include the warmer climates. Some stuff will stop working. Other stuff will be invented that makes things a bit easier or prolongs the inevitability of the changes. But ultimately, aren't we already the product of hundreds of centuries of change? The whole Earth's landmass used to be one giant island, for goodness' sake! Everything changes. This planet is a history of change. I think it's hubris to think humanity can do much to the forces already at play, and ignorance to presume that we won't be able to solve it in some way, somehow, as engineering ramps up. We are just beginning to understand how to program basic materials from scratch. Maybe one day, we will have chemical foundries that can produce industrial-scale solvents and products in a silo, and these could be anywhere in the world. We might become less and less dependent on geography and local resource limitations to supply the world's food, fuel, and needs. And maybe once everything sort of settles down and we have fusion and clean water for all and food and basic materials can be *printed*, then maybe we can start to clear out the planet's clogged arteries. I see no reason why this won't happen within the century. Therefore, I see no reason to take any draconian measures at all. We have seen the whites of the eyes and stared at the brink of extinction many times. We do so daily. We'll be fine. So yeah, basically, if our hand is under a boulder, I would very much expect to be able to move the boulder sooner than we, as a species, will perish. And so I really just ... don't know.

Maybe we will. Maybe we won't. But the evidence, as I see it, leans heavily on technological progress and an acceptance of change. We made our bed, and we will lie in it."

Seeks Authority: "And maybe I can speak up for my middle ground, centrist attitude. It's very similar to Model Builder's argument actually. I do think things are dire. I do think we are headed toward extinction. But we have a long history of rising to the occasion when it is demanded of us. We are lazy as a species in some ways and inefficient and bloody and cruel and inconsistent, but we are also insufferably persistent. And so mine is a bit of both. I think, yes, if we sat and did nothing but do what we are doing now, we would lazily cause our own extinction. But there's no way that will happen. Forces will step in. We might be dangerous, but we aren't suicidal. We will rouse the troops. We will rise. The world might look unimaginably different than it does today, but really, so what? Is this really the best version of ourselves? The richest few countries sure think so, but for the one hundred and ninety other countries and the billions of peoples still in subsistence poverty, I'd say maybe change is a good thing."

Dark Humor: "Am I the only one who is going to ask?"

Silence.

I asked, "What's on your mind, DH?"

Dark Humor: "Who the fuck is Zero, and when did he get here?"

11: Brave Old World

Q: Is Blueprint onto something?
Q: If so, how do we share it with the world?

"Actually, that is a bit strange," I said. Zero looked so familiar. I know him from somewhere, don't I? I don't remember letting him in. Somehow, though, he's here, and nobody seemed to notice or mind until Dark Humor brought it up. I gambled by speaking first. "Zero? How are you, old friend?"

Zero: "Odd. Just then, were you gambling that you knew me even though I don't quite ring a bell in your memory? As host, do you prefer pretending to know me to the alternative, that I was just *here*, suddenly, at your party?"

Dark Humor: "This is not a party, buddy. And not a public meeting, either. *Hint, hint.*"

My watch beeped. It was time for my daily walk. Just as Immanuel Kant, "the Königsberg clock," was reported to have precisely done every single day at 5 p.m. exactly.

Game Play: "Zero is with me. He came in with me. Did nobody see him? Scribe, you *really* don't recognize him?"

I replied, "Honestly, I don't. But, welcome, Zero. You know why we're here?"

Zero: "Yes, I was listening the whole time."

"Right, right," I said, slightly confused. Nobody else seemed bothered by his presence, so I didn't press it.

I asked if anyone would like to go with me on my walk. Only Zero, Blueprint, and Self Harm agreed. All said they could use the air. It was agreed that we would pick the debate back up on our return. And so we went. It was unspoken between the three of us that we needed a few minutes of shared silence to wind down. None of us seemed to even choose a direction consciously. We just walked in a random direction at each corner, like a flock of birds with no leader.

Even Self Harm couldn't bring himself to ruin the mood by breaking the silence. For my part, I was overjoyed at how well the day was going so far and allowed myself a moment to bask in it. My closest friends (plus this Zero character), together, under a single roof on this, my final day on this Earth.

And Blueprint had, though he perhaps has not yet made the *closest* friends, at least made his point of view somewhat known. I know he could go like this all day, unpacking and arguing around many of the best counterarguments. He had been evangelizing his ideas for years. They were tested and forged already by the fires of his constant contrariness and peculiarities and the way that his ideas seemed to get under people's skin immediately.

There's a saying that the fastest way to get an answer to something is to post the wrong answer to the Internet. Blueprint seemed to debate and play in the space of ideas with that same strategy sometimes.

It was also fascinating over the years watching people's conscious mind defend its own existence and survival. In one-on-one discussions, Blueprint had told me that it mostly plays provocateur to try to understand the enemy and its defenses. Certain arguments were like missile defense shields—trying to shoot down any incoming argumentative lob. And so his orneriness was on purpose. It made people want to disagree. It made them angry. It made their ideas suffused with the emotional misdirections and errors that would, to anyone paying attention, prove his very point. And, ultimately, like he had done with me, it made them eventually come around.

Blueprint and I had met years prior, sometime after the rest of us got back from the Mt. Kilimanjaro trip. We became fast friends, in part, because neither of us seemed to live in the present moment. Small talk was not only useless, but it set off both our hackles. Why would people just banter slowly when so much was going on and so much was going so poorly? There's a whole category of conversational topics that are just as inane as talking about the weather in both our views. And, yes, talking about pandemics, ongoing or otherwise, is still just talking about the weather.

We kept a tepid, friendly distance from each other in the beginning until our friendship seemed to really click at one of the famed and exclusive lunches he hosts at his place in Los

Angeles. It was a single thought experiment he had asked the table: "If you could be born anytime 500 years into the past or future, what year would it be?" That really got me thinking. The answers around the table were predictable in a *Midnight in Paris* or *Connecticut Yankee in King Arthur's Court* kind of way. Mostly they involved nostalgia for a bygone era when things "were simpler" or "when men were men" or "when there was time to think" or they wanted to sit and listen in on the Algonquin Club lunches. Nobody seemed to consider the idea that they could make *their own* Algonquin Club that people a hundred years from now would die to be at. Or that there was *plenty* of time to think if you shut out the world. My theory is that the conscious mind loves dwelling on what it knows best. Like modern AIs, it is thirsty for as much data as it can get its grubby little hands on, and so it rues the past in much more detail than the future. The past is known. The past isn't scary.

But Blueprint's answer that day alarmed me. I had tepidly chosen one hundred years into the future as my answer mostly, as I unpacked it in the following weeks, because the idea of a century is a comforting one to me. We obsessives over history talk about centuries of progress with clear enthusiasm. We say, "Turn of the century" as if it's its own object with a different set of rules and expectations. We celebrate century anniversaries with great élan. Historians write about cycles in war and disease and hope and art, all occurring in units of centuries. There are some novelists today who have submitted unread novels into a sort of time capsule that will be read, of course, one century from now. Mark Twain demanded that his autobiography only be released 100 years after his death.

To me, these all seemed related. The century is the historian's favored unit. And so, without even thinking hard on the matter, I had chosen a single century: 2120 or thereabouts. But Blueprint quickly made it clear what a silly, romantic set of logic I had used. I had tepidly chosen the least challenging of all the answers, he claimed. Interestingly, only he and I had picked a time in the future. Everyone else was in the past. And so, he harped on me the most. In part he wondered whether I chose it to be close enough that things might be recognizable but far enough into the future that things would still have progressed mightily. But he claimed that one century into the future was still far too long a time to make real sense of what was happening. Compared to 1920, for example, the mind of a 2020 human was so different that they might not even be able to talk to each other. Some things looked the same. Sure, buildings were still upright and warm and privately owned, and we lived in them and ate what appeared to be similar-looking meals. Sure, the nuclear family unit still resembled itself.

In fact, Blueprint had answered that day that what he would want to see—2540 AD—was actually outside the scope of the question by a few decades. It was the year *Brave New World* took place. Not because he wished for that world—of course, it is a world of pure nightmare—but because he wanted more data on the way in which predictions about the future could be right or wrong and about the stories humans tell each other.

And so, he said he would choose a year as far into the future as the time traveler/experimenter allowed: 500 years.

Immediately, I realized his answer was the correct one.

I was tickled imagining it. Think only, he had said, about the change across the world between 1520 and 2020. It was hard to imagine. Magellan had just become the first to cross from the Atlantic to the Pacific. Vast, vast tracts of the Earth were still unexplored. Martin Luther had posted his theses only three years prior. You could bump into Renaissance greats in the right cafe. The *David*, *Mona Lisa*, and the roof of the Sistine Chapel were considered modern art. With intrepid sleuthing, you could buy or at least find a copy of Gutenberg's Bible, fresh off his printing press, only a few decades old. Ideas were brewing in English cafés, too: Shakespeare, Marlowe, and Spenser would write their works in the coming decades. Monarchy and theocracy ruled the world.

Thinking about what the world had been through in the last 500 years gave me shivers. Imagining what it would go through in the *next* 500 years left me pale. And so I came to see that he was perhaps on to something. It was a fascinating inversion of the psychological principle of temporal discounting. Most people, most of the time, perceive things in the far future as less valuable than things closer to the present. It's so common it is almost a universal rule of psychology, as close as they get to a capital-L Law.

The simplest version is: Would you rather have $100 now or $500 in one month? How about $500 in one year? Ten years? One century from now? Every other version is really just a variant of that idea to try to get at some sort of equivalency. What it and questions like it do, when you do them over a single person with hundreds of variants or over hundreds of people with just one scenario, is give data to the exchange rate of time itself. If there are different answers to different values at different time points, which there of course are, then you can start to view time as a variable or multiplier or even more interestingly as a kind of currency itself.

The unit "one year" in the future is not just a strict multiplier for value but can be best thought of in the economic modeling sense as a different country with a global exchange rate just like any other. And by far, almost universally, the further away in time the thing is, the more it is discounted, forward or backward. Mostly forward. The reason is straightforward. In any explore-exploit paradigm, like with decision-making, the structure of the equations and equivalencies are all related to how one views or values future rewards. It gets even messier when the future reward is unknown or probabilistic, as it seems to be in Blueprint's thought experiment. The future is *unknown*. The past is *known*. And so, said Blueprint, two things seem to be going on when people answer the question by claiming they would wish to be in the past. They discount both the future and discount the unknown, as if two storm fronts combined into a severe cognitive weather pattern muddying the rational waters. Of course, people had their common rebuttals. They said that they couldn't know whether or not the world *will even exist* in 500 years, so the expected value of that weighed against the likelihood that life will get better isn't a negligible factor. Who knows what the world will be like, they said. Dusty and apocalyptic? Overrun by AI overlords?

"*Exactly*," Blueprint had said.

He had done his Socratic magic trick yet again. He had gotten people to start to envision the possible bleakness of the future and admit that in their answer to this one, seemingly unrelated question, they were actually revealing both the amount in which they discounted the future *and* their hidden beliefs about whether they think humanity is headed toward its extinction or not. This he then proposed as Blueprint's wager, a bit like a modified Pascal's wager. He went even further with the definition, which said that if anyone answered that they would travel to the past in the 500-year hypothetical because, in part, they were unsure whether the future will hold an Earth worth living in, then *no matter how slim the percentage chance* they saw of that future unfolding, it is rational to give it their all today, in this brief life, as if it had a 100 percent chance of occurring.

Like Pascal's wager, which posited that no matter how slim the chance of there being an afterlife, it is at least nonzero, and therefore there is no real harm in being a devout believer. *Just in case.* Well, said Blueprint, how different is the logic really when confronting the annihilation of our entire species?

It was that moment when I realized what Blueprint was getting at with what appeared, at first, to be just a vain, anti-aging agenda of someone who lost their religion and needed to pick up the emotional pieces of the wreckage. No, it was much bigger than that. He was in the middle of the biggest magic trick he would ever pull: trying to get people to have individual and bodily familiarity with sensors, feedback loops, and the rigors of what it really takes to reverse something as impossibly unidirectional seeming as *biological aging* ... as the first step in reversing something as impossibly unidirectional seeming as climate change or whatever plagues our future.

The strategy was, I came to believe, a sound one. People have all kinds of ways of thinking about the future, the past, danger, and the expected values or expected risks of technologies. If you truly unpacked all the possible varieties of ways to consider how people construct moral and existential arguments, there was no hope of ever getting people to agree based on a third party, external arguments alone. What it took was for each person to have their aha moment on their own, but they would only get there by first having experience with the Blueprint diet and health agenda. *Only then would they truly understand that what appears to be irreversible is in fact reversible.* It was never actually about age or vanity or telomeres or skin spots. The protocol is simply a proving ground for doing battle with the impossible.

Only then would people realize that the only way to change certain biological trends is discipline, lifestyle, and asceticism. Only then would they come to understand that unimagined joy and contentment exists on the other side of the cognitive bias electrified fence hemming them in. Only then would they truly understand that our decision-making was not meant to handle decisions on the scale of the entire planet because the causal forces are impossible for any one mind to gather and hold in its mind's eye at once. And that, because of all this, and in order to mitigate against the slight chance that we *don't* solve much of what plagues us today, we need to presume that things won't be solved by default and therefore have every moral duty and obligation to act now, as if humanity will lose Blueprint's wager, and have the serious and difficult discussions now about what, if anything, to change or sacrifice for the greater good of the future. The cost of losing the wager is too great.

And so, around that day, as I couldn't stop thinking about the conversations from lunch, I became a convert. Not per se to the exact or rigid protocols Blueprint adheres to in his daily life—he can be the Ernest Shackleton figure, for all I care, exploring his South Pole and losing his toes—but because I do buy the underlying premise that, for some inexplicable reason, people do not seem to see the looming danger. We are privy to the whims of a brain that has a much easier time imagining a comet destroying Earth than slow, gradual change. We are the frog boiling in the pot, and only by a careful, narrow, and considered recognition that we have cognitive blind spots will we advance beyond them to land at real, actionable solutions. All of this, remarkably, I had gathered from just a few minutes of lovely, but difficult and charged, debate at Blueprint's home.

Before I knew it, we were back at the house.

Half an hour had passed, and not a single word was said between us on our walk. The four of us had been entirely silent, each lost in thought. Even Self Harm kept to himself. He cleared his throat a few times as if he was about to say something but ultimately never did.

Blueprint: "I just figured something out."

"Oh," I said. "What is that?"

Blueprint: "How to respond to the *Brave New World* argument. Emotions can coexist with the full extent of human thriving. In fact, they are essential to it. The book misunderstood that."

I said, "Honestly, I had expected more of a methodological comeback. I'm surprised to hear that you seemed to take the arguments to heart. I expected you to say something like, 'Well, as we can see from the kinds of assumptions *Brave New World* makes about the future, things are just as they were, except slightly different. Yes, true, it's a book full of traffic jams. It's a brilliant exercise in how different society can be if we tweak just a few things, like how children are made and raised. It's a brilliant exercise in how different things could be if we put Earth in the wrong hands. But it's a failure in creativity. It does not predict anything beyond what already existed in the first half of the twentieth century. Things are similar. Babies are still babies. Tennis is just a slightly different kind of tennis. People still sleep like people sleep just with radios playing in their ears to indoctrinate them. The robots don't run anything. It's not a realistic vision of a world with five hundred years of difference. Everything will be so unimaginably different.'"

Blueprint: "Sure, I could have said those things, but I figured someone else or maybe even everybody would get there on their own. No, I have a much deeper thing to say about people's base worries."

And with that, Blueprint opened the door.

We were greeted with a *very* surprise guest.

Depression, looking only a little worse for wear since last I saw him, was standing in the doorway and removing his shoes.

12: Shades of Blue

Q: Will Depression ruin everything?
Q: Again?

Dark Humor, as always, was *on* it. He was good for many things, the most useful being his ability to immediately cut the tension in any room.

Dark Humor: "Depression. Old pal. Showing up out of nowhere after everybody thought you were dead? A little on the nose, isn't it? Makes sense that you couldn't even be the first to do that. We're still getting over the surprise of Zero over here."

Zero: "I've been here the whole time."

Depression's voice was soft and ruffled, like he hadn't spoken in months: "Love you too, DH."

Most others in the room had frozen solid. Except for Cognitive Bias, who got up to give Depression a hug, and Seeks Authority, who immediately walked straight past the commotion and fled through the back door. They had a lot of history and back story, those two—Depression had both been Seeks Authority's best friend and then bully at some point in their adolescence.

"It's not out of nowhere," I said. "I invited him."

Dark Humor was still the only one who could speak. There was a certain utility to not caring a lick what others thought.

Dark Humor: "I thought you were dead."

Devil May Care: "So did I."

Depression: "You were all worried you killed me, right? Left me to die on the mountain?"

Game Play: "I wouldn't say 'worried' is the most accurate word." He, too, had had a falling out with Depression years back. They had tried to start a business together in their twenties, but Game Play's view on the world soured markedly during their time together as partners. The apathy and anhedonia had spread to Game Play's sense of joy, popping it like a balloon once their efforts had started flagging.

Blueprint, though, could only smile at the surprise presence of Depression. Without pause, he walked up and shook Depression's hand, like any other warm welcome.

Blueprint: "I'm Blueprint. I've heard a lot about you. Not all of it good, but most of it good. I am truly happy to see you here today. Thank you for coming."

The tone was set. Depression would not be a pariah. Or, perhaps, Blueprint just had no idea how bad things could get.

Dark Humor: "Half the room looks like they see a ghost." It was true. Many had paled, speechless.

Depression: "Anyone have a drink?"

Devil May Care: "Sure do, buddy. Was glad somebody asked. I'll get another one. I mean I'll get you one. I mean I'll get one."

Depression: "Thanks." He was oscillating between confidence and worry with his posture, I could tell. He wasn't sure how the room would receive him. If the room was entirely warm, that would have been the worst case because everyone would both have been faking it, and even worse, everyone would *know* they and all the others were faking it, including Depression. And even if the response was universally cold, Depression at least knew how to handle that. It's how life was most of the time through his eyes. But this sort of tepid, divided response was almost as bad as the worst case.

People were forming groups about whether to like or dislike, approve or disapprove of his presence, which only left him tired from trying to navigate the perceived group disputes and borderlines. He would much rather it be him vs. the room. At least then the enemies would be clear, and he would know nobody from his side would turn on him because, like with most of the time, nobody was on his side.

I saw this all play out and knew that I had more say today than perhaps I ever had and certainly ever again would.

I said, "Depression is here as my guest and our friend. I heard some rumors that he had made it off the mountain eventually, rescued by Sherpas, and healed in Nepal for a few months before returning back here and basically hiding from us for a while. Pretending to be dead, I suppose?"

Depression, grabbing the beer Devil May Care had kindly procured for him: "What's the difference?" Devil May Care smiled and clinked his bottle to Depression's. Thus, the first truce was called.

"Does anybody object to Depression being here?" I asked.

Silence.

Model Builder: "I don't object. But I would like to get something off my chest. I've changed a lot since I last saw you, Depression, and I've done a lot of soul searching in the meantime about what happened on the mountain. I've even done some research on the anthropological or social need for someone like you in any group setting. Here's what I'm working with. We all have our different ways of approaching the world, and what I've tried so hard to understand is, basically, why you still exist. I didn't quite understand it. Not you as an individual, Depression. You have your own personal quirks and flaws, and we love you for them as much as we ... find it difficult, sometimes, to have you around. You know that. I'm sorry if I'm bringing up old wounds. But the question that kept me up at night for weeks after getting off that mountain is, why does the kind of person you are still exist in modern man? Because, to be honest, you almost got us killed up there. You know that. That's hard to forgive. And so the paradox in my mind has been trying to resolve whether or not there are essential features to your existence that actually are positive in some lights or some of the time. There has to be a reason for your doom and gloom, right?

"The analog is that I've found all kinds of pseudo-explanations for how or why other kinds of divergent thinking came to survive until now, with the idea that different kinds of minds or personalities exist because there was some evo-lutionary benefit somewhere along the way. The attention deficit–disordered brain is good for foraging in new places. The novelty-seeking brain is good for tribal expansion. The person with phobias of the unknown is good for taking care of the nesting at home. The super autobiographical memory folk might know where the watering hole is. The schizophrenic or schizotypal brain is selected because of its utility as a shaman, mystic, or leader. Etc., etc. The idea being that all the kinds of diversity or difference that we see is here, in a sense, because there's been a need for each and every type of brain in order to achieve robust adaptability of any group. There are of course maladaptations occasionally, like there are with so many genes and traits throughout the mammalian and biological world. That's not what I mean here, though. The question I most want to hear *you* answer first, before we even get to talking about what you did on that mountain, is: 'Why do you think you're useful, Depression?' I'm sorry that's so blunt. I've been wanting to ask you about it for years. I have my own answer, but I'd love to hear yours first."

Depression: "I'd be happy to hear your answer first, actually."

Game Play: "I'd rather you go first."

Depression: "Oh, I heard you. I'm afraid, though, I don't actually owe you that. If you want the debate, you might as well start it off. Shouldn't be any harder than summiting."

"Boys, boys," I said. "Game Play, since you brought it up, that does seem fair. Why don't you continue with what's on your mind."

Game Play paced for a moment. We all knew he had the next word, no matter how long it took.

Game Play: "All right, so the most important trait in anything victim to the whims of evolution is adaptability. Evolution is survival of the survivors, not survival of the most beautiful, elegant, or fit. 'Fitness' is a bit of an outdated term. 'Adaptability' has taken its throne, and all the Darwin coffee mugs and bumper stickers should all say, 'Survival of the Adaptable-est' or whatever the phrase is, right? So how does a mood or mind like Depression's fit in? It must, right? I've long wondered about various diseases and mental illnesses and whether their existence is inevitable or just a kind of evolutionary fluke. Think about cancer, maybe, as an analogy. There was Ice Age cancer. We know this. All mammals can get it. It's neither uniquely human nor uniquely modern. But the modern way of life *greatly increases* the kinds, severity, and frequency of many cancers. What this means is that there is some rationale to saying that cancer is a modern disease, but what we really mean by this statement is, 'Relative to the normalized rates of cancer expected from simply living a subsistence, natural life as a biological creature on this planet, the high rates of cancer today are a modern disease.' Which is to say: cancer is not a modern disease. *But the rates of it are.*

"Or we might ask a similar question about dementia. Is dementia a modern or ancient disease? We live longer now, which makes the development of dementia more likely and acts as a confound. So it's a bit of a false question. Cells have always degraded when they are overworked, and the brain is just a bunch of cells degrading together because we're basically just an overclocked ape. So dementia isn't evolutionarily adapted in any strict sense but is a necessary consequence of *another* physical and cognitive trait—memory—which is adaptive. It's the other side of the coin. And this is what I've been wrestling with all these years. The possible categories are set—either something is a directly adaptive trait, like ADHD or foraging. Or it is the flip side of the coin of some *other* trait that *does* contribute to the adaptability of the individual and therefore the tribe. So which is it? My guess, after thinking it through for a while, and of course while trying to work through what happened on the mountain, is that Depression isn't adaptive directly. I think it's a sequela. Shadow. A maladaptive curse, inevitable in a small percent of people for some reason because the mild version is actually the seat of imagination itself, or something."

Depression: "If I wasn't so used to your aimless blathering, I do think I might consider that I might be insulted by those statements, GP. I mean, I wasn't exactly expecting silver balloons and strippers popping out of cakes, but if this is all the welcome greeting I get, I'll take it. I still missed you guys. Despite, you know."

I said, "There are mentions of deep melancholy in texts throughout history. Ancient Egypt. Pliny. Medieval manuscripts. If it's maladaptive, as you say, Game Play, it sure is common."

Zero: "So is cancer. You'll find it anywhere you find life."

Model Builder: "Anywhere you find *long-term* life. It's the trade-off evolution has accepted between complex life and the machine occasionally breaking down."

Depression: "That's what they say."

Blueprint started to say something, made the hints of stirring noises that indicated he wanted the room. But something made him pause.

"Blueprint?" I asked. Sometimes such simple goading worked. I never quite understood why it worked even with the smartest people I knew. Social approval? Inertia? The simple re-asking of a question did wonders for fluidity and getting some people unstuck. But Blueprint didn't ever need to be unstuck. There was always a reason.

Blueprint: "I'm thinking Game Play's concerns through. I'm not at an answer yet, though."

"That doesn't stop most of us," I said.

Blueprint: "Fair. I can say what I have so far. But can I first ask Game Play a question? How do you determine whether an observed trait in a modern human is 'directly adaptive,' as you say, or simply an inevitable trade-off as a consequence of a separate trait? What evidence do you have about the evolutionary fitness of one thing or another except a kind of plausible story about what may or may not have happened long ago? Every culture that has been carefully studied has someone like Depression in it, from the !Kung of southern Africa to the Ache of Paraguay to every culture about which we've ever had written records. And even comparative biology seems to back up the idea that the receptors that underlie depressive feelings, or at the very least that are targeted by drugs that alleviate such feelings, are highly conserved across many animals including mice and monkeys and all the ones close to us. That means that something might be going on with Depression that is more than just a maladaptive accident. Maybe, for example, there is a certain cognitive outlook that Depression brings that is useful at times. Maybe they are rare times. Or maybe they aren't as rare as we would like to hope."

Game Play: "Well, you can't just say that because something is still around and was or is useful in certain narrow circumstances means it has to be a good thing. There used to be no oxygen on the planet. We all have weird-ass extracranial pineal organs that are light sensitive but tucked away inside our brains now because they aren't useful. They used to detect light, like a crude eye. But now they're just shoved into the middle of the skull like a winter jacket that's never worn. This organ is 'still around' but useless. Just because something still exists and just because a trait has a niche for it to be useful doesn't mean those conditions exist anymore or ever will again."

Zero: "And what if they did?"

Game Play: "Meaning?"

Zero: "Meaning, for example, that maybe the future will hold humanity in an unexpected vice grip, and maybe whatever the underlying features are to the *cognitive* impact of depression— not the emotional or physical, mind you, which are a tougher sell—but perhaps the ruminations and obsessions and analytical lens are useful in narrow ways. Perhaps the desire for isolation is an early anti-germ strategy. There are studies that depressed people are better at solving social problems. That if they tend to self-describe becoming depressed during challenging tasks that require perseveration, they score higher. That depressed people are better than non-depressed people at accurately counting how many bad guys they jumped on in a video game. It's called 'depressive realism.' The idea is that maybe, just maybe, the default way of seeing the word is skewed slightly optimistic, which means that if you want an accurate accounting of affairs, social or intellectual, maybe Depression is your guy."

Devil May Care sat with a big smile on his face. He may not have forgiven Depression for Mount Kilimanjaro, but he clearly respected what Blueprint and Zero were trying to do. Self Critical also seemed cheered by Depression's presence. They had always got along when push came to shove. In fact, they often echoed each other. Farm Boy, I could tell, was highly bothered by Blueprint's attempts. His arms were crossed, and he was staring at Depression, squinting, like at a fire he had to watch slowly burn out. Seeks Authority was still outside. The biggest surprise was Cognitive Bias, who seemed delighted at the combined novelty and nostalgia of having an old friend appear again. Depression seemed to be enjoying the attention. He was, though I may have lost count, already on the second beer.

Model Builder: "But we don't know evolution's full playground. And we can't ever know. We just can't re-create it, and so we're just conjecturing."

Blueprint: "And that's precisely it. If we cannot simulate the exact conditions or terrain or detail on which evolution plays out, and if there are any positive aspects at all to the trait, then we have no result other than concluding that Depression is in fact an essential part of group *dynamics*, if not group cohesion. And further that it—he—is highly adaptive in certain circumstances where too much Pollyanna-esque optimism is blinding. On top of a mountain, facing certain death, seems like exactly one of those scenarios."

Relentless: "Watch it. You weren't there."

Blueprint: "No, I wasn't. But the very fact that you all made it argues to me that Depression's role might have been essential to some part of the journey that aided in survival. Perhaps even just the act of sloughing him off gave the group a kind of cohesion it would never otherwise have. Perhaps you are all familiar with the psychology study in the 1950s where they took two groups of boys, none of whom knew each other, and divided them *randomly* into two teams. If you aren't familiar, the TL;DR is that things got bad, quick. They got so violent toward the other group after a few competitive exercises for resources in their arbitrary groupings that the whole experiment almost got turned off. Big red emergency STOP button. But the experimenters had an idea. They next introduced an imaginary third group, the 'vandals,' and lo and behold it made the initial two groups bond together instantly and work together against this new foreign threat. You mean to say someone is coming for the resources *we* are fighting over?! *How dare they.* You may see where I'm going with this. It sounds paradoxical. It sounds like it can't possibly be true on its face. But maybe the evolutionarily adaptive benefit to having Depression in any group, and in your friend group even, is that it operates like an internal vandal, giving the rest of the group something to rally around and against. To define oneself around and against. Case in point: you guys aren't even all friends anymore, right? You used to be a close group. Now, many of you hadn't seen each other for years until today. You can give all kinds of explanations for why, and some of them might be valid in part, but have you considered the fact that you miss Depression? That you *needed* him?"

Dark Humor: "This sounds like something I would be saying. As satire." He paused, with a mimic of Rodin's *The Thinker* pose, theatrically, before continuing. "But I do like to say my satire only works because it's mostly true, so, well, I guess I agree, Blueprint."

Zero: "On our walk just now, outside, with Seeks Authority and Scribe, I got to thinking about the question about how similar at first glance a pitch for a world of automation in certain decision-making—and, therefore, an intentional de-motion of the conscious mind—is to *Brave New World*. The abstract and descriptive words for both do, at first glance, appear similar. 'Automation,' 'demotion of will,' etc. But thanks to the discussion earlier, I have realized a key difference."

He did this often. Or at least, I had seen him do it a few times already in debate or at his lunches. Long after he had already come to a conclusion on his own, he presented it, as if thinking through it aloud, as a deliberate contemplation of an overturned belief of his own influenced by the arguments of the day. The exact phrase seemed even to repeat itself: "Thanks to the discussion earlier, I have realized a key difference." It meant, excitingly, that he was about to drop an argumentative hammer.

Depression: "I love how useful I'm being, just sitting here doing nothing. Clearly this is my calling. DMC, are we out?"

Devil May Care: "Sadly, yes."

Zero: "I can start with the grandest version of the claim, as I hear it being argued. I even agree. In fact, it is my considered opinion that without depression, the world would have already ended."

I couldn't tell if this was one of his rhetorical tricks or not. It certainly seemed too provocative to be easily backed up.

Depression: "Amen. This is the best family reunion I've ever attended. I like these new guys, too."

Zero: "Let me explain. In *Brave New World*, emotions are mostly eliminated or managed with soma, right, the sort of all-purpose, panacea of a wonder drug. Precisely what's missing, and precisely why the world is the dystopia it is, is because Depression here is missing. Think of each personality trait we have like a Jenga tower. You all know the game, right? Stack wooden planks on top of each other, and then remove them one by one until the tower collapses. Imagine a person is a huge Jenga tower with thousands of pieces. And written on each wooden block, on the face that faces out, is a personality trait. Compassion. Ambition. Self-consciousness. Extroversion. Introversion. Libido. Desire for novelty. Humor. Here's the important part: if you are standing and staring at a single face of the Jenga tower and all you see is one trait you don't like— say, Depression—and if you push that piece out, what happens? *You also lose whatever trait was on the other side of the piece.* Forget what you were saying a bit ago, Game Play, about the fact that we'll never be able to fully re-create the conditions in which evolution forged us. More importantly, we can't always know, from our point of view, which only sees one side, what traits or cognitive features of a person are linked on the other side of the Jenga block. Let's say you wanted a partner or friend to be less self-conscious. So you find the 'self-conscious' Jenga block and push it out. But guess what's on the other side of that? *Because* they were self-conscious, say, they had taken it upon themselves to be wildly ambitious for the sake of balancing out a perceived lack that they thought they had. *Because* they were X, they became Y. And so what's on the other side of the Jenga piece for Depression? I claim that the Jenga piece for Depression has on its other face ... Cohesion. Unity. Depression is not the fire. He's the fire alarm telling the group that something is *very wrong.* But before we go any further, do you mind if I ask you all a question? Do any of you have any idea how old you are?"

13: Is Age Reversible?

Q: Can we rewrite the operating system of our bodies?
Q: Of our minds?

I admit it. I was confused.

"And you mean by that ...?" I asked.

I was speaking about the question I knew the rest of the room had swirling in their minds. It was my party, after all, and I could be the town crier if I wanted to. Blueprint and Zero started answering for each other. They were going to get along just fine, it seems.

Blueprint: "He means, and I wonder, if anybody has noticed a change in the rate of their aging in the last few years, since the last time you all saw Depression?"

Game Play: "That's not how age works," said Game Play. He appeared to still be irked that Depression and Blueprint had mostly, in their recent answers, misdirected everyone from his arguments from a bit ago. Nobody had seemed to directly answer his query about direct adaptability.

Blueprint: "Oh, but it is." He put a comforting hand on Depression's shoulder. "The concept of depression—not you, new friend, but the general idea of it—is known to accelerate all kinds of cellular and biological markers of aging. It accelerates heart disease, cancer, diabetes. On the senescence-associated secretory phenotype, which is a kind of composite puzzle of lots of different pieces—cytokines, tissue, temperature, growth factors, all kinds of things—things get a lot worse with depression. Everything does. It's a system-wide assault on every cell in the body. And its final form, suicide, of course, is life at *the most* accelerated kind of aging. The rapidest of rapid cliffs to fall off. No pun intended."

He was being too blunt. Losing the room.

Cognitive Bias, of all people, seemed to see through Blueprint's plan.

Cognitive Bias: "I don't think we need to go back here, Blueprint. I get it. Time's arrow. One way. Scribe was hinting to me earlier about your plan here. Aging is supposed to be a one-way street, and you are here to tell us it's not. You are here to tell us that the inevitable heat death of the universe is *not* a given. That you can turn water into wine. That you found the Fountain, and it's been *inside us all along*. Oh, joy. That you and you alone can bring every cell in a body to the promised land, right? I'm being sarcastic, if you can't tell."

Blueprint: "Yes, we can tell. I think maybe you've mis-understood me, CB. Maybe everyone here has. Scribe, do you know why I do all this health and wellness stuff? Do you think I *want* to live forever?"

196

"I have my guesses as to why. But I don't actually know, no," I said.

Blueprint: "Well, it's because I know the burden of having a Depression in one's life. I know what it's like to have your least-favorite friend show up at the party at random times. I know what it's like to be at the top of a mountain—figurative or literal, doesn't matter—and have every ounce of your non-exhausted being contemplate chucking yourself off the side of the mountain. And that's when it hit me a few years ago, right before I got into all this. Depression is not a disease of serotonin. It's not an imbalance of humors. It's not where vitality goes to die. *It's a disease of accelerated aging.* This is not its side effect. This is its core purpose. Game Play, to your earlier question, which I guess by now you've given up on us truly answering—yes, of course, *it is adaptive.* It's a culling mechanism turned sour but a useful one. Joy slows down time. Depression speeds it up. That's it. The 'sadness' or darkness or whatever people think is the core nature of the disease is not the core nature of the disease. The sadness is a mere side effect."

Depression: "So, what, let me spell this out if I can." He seemed unbothered, as always. "I'm staring at the clock right now. And I'm here in the room. It seems to be moving as clocks do—one second at a time. Nothing seems to be accelerating. There's no blue shift for aging, so to speak, merely by my very existence."

Blueprint: "It's not happening to the outside world's clocks. It's happening to all the clocks on each and every one of our insides. The presence of someone like you changes the very programming of cells to speed up to their ultimate fate, like an audiobook at one-point-twenty-five-x speed. And here's what they don't tell you. Nobody will. No amount of antidepressant on the planet reverses that. That's not what they do, and that's not what they're for. People's need to see the disease as an imbalance in neurotransmitter X is a century-long red herring. It is a disease of aging. When it happens, it happens faster."

Farm Boy: "So you're saying even though we survived our trip to the top of Mt. K, we all were artificially older when we came back?"

Blueprint: "Like the opposite of going at relativistic speeds, near the speed of light, yes. One way you might consider thinking about our pal Depression here is that, if you are traveling at a velocity close to the speed of light, you do technically slow down relative to anything not traveling near the speed of light. We know this is part of the NASA twin experiments, where the twinned astronaut who went into space came back *slightly* younger than his twin who stayed on Earth. We're talking picoseconds here. Nanoseconds. But it's measurable, nonetheless. And fascinating. And so, what I'm saying is that, yes, merely being in the same room as Depression here is aging us all *as if we had relativistically slowed down*. The best definition of having Depression around is, physically and physiologically, lowering the average velocity of particles in the room. In any closed system, really."

Model Builder: "I'm sure, and I can forgive you, but you're speaking poetically, right? I sort of get the trope about aging slower than others if you are traveling close to the speed of light, but anything in the realm of the timescales of cells or life or biology isn't happening at either quantum or relativistic speeds. There is no superfast or super-slow relevant to a cell just doing cellular things. Like the clock on the wall."

Cognitive Bias: "But the clock on the wall *does* speed or slow down depending on how fast you're traveling, technically. Right? I might not be too good at too many things, but I *am* good at understanding what it means for your worldview to have rules separate from everybody else's. In fact, that's the basis for a new existential philosophy I'm developing. Maybe if I could—"

Nobody wanted to hear it. It would be riddled with so-called "ostrich effects" anyway—CB with his head in the sand, ignoring anything that contradicted his worldview. Model Builder interrupted him before he went too far, as had happened many times throughout the years. He was CB's de facto conver- sational wrangler.

Model Builder: "I find it hard to believe that senescent clocks and real-world analog clocks are operating under the same rules. I see your point, Blueprint, that age can be, oh, I don't know, slowed a bit. But we're not talking about slowing any actual biology. It's just a cellular physiology thing, isn't it? Like how people can die if they don't sleep for a week or so. It's just waste disposal. Our older cells are like hoarders who need their debris removed. And it needs to be removed constantly or else, *croak*." He made a gesture across his throat with his thumb. A dramatic one. "All kinds of things can 'age' us rapidly, as you say. Make us fall rapidly off the cliff. One and a half or two minutes, *tops* ... that's how often we need a full resupply of oxygen from our macroenvironment. By which I mean our planet. How insane is that? Literally every few seconds we need a resupply. That's so often! Why? Why can't our lungs be larger? Why haven't we figured out the right razor's edge of cognition so that we live a thousand years and don't die of all these silly things like cancer, stroke, and cardiovascular disease? It's ridiculous."

"You seem to be railing against the sky, Model Builder," I said.

Model Builder: "I am. It seems unfair that we are so fragile. And I see no other alternative than to take all these facts and realize that aging is inevitable and one way and is a necessary, direct consequence of the biological needs we have. We run too hot. We need too much debris clearing. Someone made this trade for us. We didn't choose it. There's no other way. Aging is an essential part of being alive. You can't reverse it. Arrow of time, second law of thermodynamics. These are not mutable. They are facts of the universe. We are going one way and one way only."

Blueprint: "And you'd stake your life on that?"

Model Builder: "I am already fully invested, yes. I see no alternative."

Blueprint: "But don't you see that Depression *is* the existence proof that more is possible?"

Model Builder: "I'm sorry, how?"

Zero took his chance, interrupted: "Look, I'm with Blueprint here, I must say. Imagine we are in, oh, 1901. The nineteenth century is behind us. We have one hundred years of the twentieth century in front of us. Electricity is new. Cars and flight are whispered about but still sort of impossible. Physicists and philosophers are brimming with excitement about having solved gases and thermodynamics and things like that. What couldn't they imagine? At the very least, they imagined that flight might *one day* be possible. They had stories about going to the Moon. Why wouldn't they? It's just up. Our explorers have gone to where they can see or where they know they can one day see. We follow our eyelines to our manifest destiny fates, right? Everyone can look up and imagine, 'I want to go up.' What they couldn't imagine was that the entire physical world around them would one day be ruled by little programmable machines. The twentieth century was the century of *programming.* It was the century of the software compiler and the hardware transistor. The explosion in human capability brought on by the programmability of our physical universe is so monumental as to be uncountable. We are still tallying the benefits, and we will likely never stop, as by the time you're done pausing, the world has already moved beyond what could previously be counted. And the point is that if you asked someone in 1901 what they would imagine could be done with a fully programmable physical microchip, they would tell you that maybe they could make *nineteenth century problems* slightly more efficient. They would tell you that maybe people will program light bulbs. Maybe they will one day have self-driving telegrams. People would bemoan the lack of telegraph operator jobs and the *New York Times* would cover their side of the lamentations about the economy and how entire cities would be made obsolete by automated telegraphs, and absolutely nobody would tell you that in one hundred years teenagers would be sitting in front of programmable light boxes with their hands on programmable controllers as they dabbled with avatars in a fully programmable software universe made by Nintendo, the playing card start-up from Japan founded in 1889. See what I mean? What toy 'playing card' company was founded in 1989 that we entirely ignore right now but will dominate the programmable future at the turn of the twenty-first century? What will bring that about?"

Blueprint: "Programmable biology."

"Exactly," I said. "Say more, if you can, Blueprint."

Blueprint: "Yeah, so Scribe is onto something here. It's a good analogy. It's not correct to say the past century was the century of physics. It was the century of *programmable physics*. Likewise, the twenty-first century is going to be the century of *programmable biology*. It's already here in pieces. We've had our Wright Brothers moments. The sequencing of the human genome was probably the analog to that. How long did it take to go from that to the Moon? Sixty years? So what will genomes be like in sixty years? Unimaginably different from 1999, when the genome was first fully sequenced. And just like flight, which is a *fight against the laws of nature and gravity*, we will be able to print proteins, design proteins, create artificial telomerases and enzymes and the like. We will be able to fully program our present, our future, and our biological destiny.

"And we sit here, asking what that might look like. And the problem is, *we have no idea*. I spend most of every day of my life thinking about what I truly know today about the body and mind from first principles, and I must say, it's very little. It's a lot, sure. A cell biology textbook in a random campus bookstore contains about a thousand years of accumulated, condensed knowledge. Why these books don't outsell the Bible is beyond me. They are how things *actually* work. But it's still *nothing* compared to what we will know about how things work one century from now, which is nothing compared to what we will know five centuries from now. It's thrilling. But the point is that we cannot even begin to imagine the tools available, and maybe even at the consumer level, to our future selves. We will put together organisms the way we put together Lego sets now. Kids will have genetic engineering kits under their Christmas trees every year with instructions, just like the Lego sets of today, to turn them into any number of possible creatures or machines. But that's only the beginning. Once we can program our biology on the microscale, we can start *large* bioengineering projects. We didn't used to be able to move mountains or build dams or clear mountains or blast islands into nuclear smithereens. Large-scale terraforming and geoengineering have made staggering leaps in ability, right? We went from tilling a field to being able to redirect the Mississippi and make fusion reactions five times hotter than the center of the Sun.

"Shortly, and I believe the day is soon, we will have biological programming on the micro *and macro* scales. The micro is what we can easily imagine. We can get inside cells and tinker with the fates and weakness and build maybe some synthetic enzymes or maybe some sort of programmable thyroid or immune cells so that we can *upload* vaccines like we do with firmware updates instead of the medieval annual shots that we have to take. Not to mention that mRNA vaccines are already here. People don't realize that the technologies behind mRNA vaccines and CRISPR are the equivalent to the transistor for computers. That the 'personal computer' will happen for biology one day too. You will have an activity monitor that tells you what's going on. You will have APIs and programmable languages using human-readable and human-writable abstraction layers that you can tap into to control your circadian rhythms and your peak mental or physical performance. They will circulate in your blood and brain and be in every organ system and tell you about the slightest arrhythmia. They will tell you when you need protein X from plant Y or a certain number of milligrams of nutrient Z."

He paused for a second while he paced the room. "And that this revolution will coincide with an explosion in the capabilities of our AI systems as well as, probably—probably—massive, game-changing breakthroughs in energy generation and extraction, and suddenly, you can start to see the pieces coming together. The level of inflammation in your body will be displayed as easily as taking your temperature or blood pressure right now. Getting your brain scanned will be as easy as taking a glucose reading. It will happen without you even knowing. The programmable systems embedded throughout the body will be ready and willing, alongside or built with advanced AI ... and when I say, 'advanced,' I mean, *unrecognizable* to us today ... and everything is going to be different. But like those people in 1901 unable to imagine just how programmable things will get, so too is it impossible for us, today, to imagine how wildly, creatively, and massively programmable the future of life on this planet is going to be. We are going to be able to *print food*. Do you realize how much of our world right now is dedicated to shuttling energy around, either as food or in unrefined energy or materials? It's insane. It's ninety percent of everything. A huge chunk of our entire global economy is just shuttling proteins or stored electrons from one side of the world to another. That will all go away when you can print proteins on demand. That will all go away when advanced AI—remember, this means AI as unimaginably advanced to us as Apollo 11 would have looked to the Wright Brothers—has had its mind put to the tasks of nuclear fusion and mathematics and the statistics of how cells and minds work. We might not even know how they do it, but such AI *will* give us the tools to one day intervene and reverse what we think of as inevitable processes."

Farm Boy: "Hold on. If I may interrupt, Blueprint. I'm listening, but I'm stuck on one point. Print ... proteins? You mean, get rid of farms?"

Blueprint: "Don't take it personally, old boy, but yes. You're the telegram operator of the twentieth century. You are, or will be one day, outdated. Technology almost always aims first at the means of production. Food feeds the world. Every ancient and even modern civilization has sprouted around rivers because we need water, and we need transportation of goods. That's it. That's why every river in the world, even in the goddamn Amazon or Congo, is scribbled in with *H. sapiens* all along. It's because we still count on nature to do the programming for us. We have inherited nature's operating system. But we thought that was true in the 1800s also. The smartest and best scientists all thought they had solved it all. There was even a German scientist, Max Schultze, who was dying, and on his deathbed said, 'All the important questions … had now been settled … except the eel question.'"

Farm Boy: "The '*Eel question*'?" He didn't know. Nobody knew what Blueprint meant. He would surely have explained eventually, right?

Blueprint: "Yeah, nobody had ever seen a baby eel at the time, I think. They appeared sui generis. Like how most people alive today have never seen a baby seagull. But they don't ever wonder why. We've stopped confronting our most basic mysteries, haven't we? Anyway, at the time, back then, scuba wasn't really a thing, so nobody knew where eels came from. Just that they appeared in the oceans and terrified everyone. The point is more the first part of the sentence: 'All the important questions … had now been settled.' Every generation seems to think that, unable to imagine the unimaginable. But you *can* imagine the unimaginable if you train hard enough. It's not easy, but it can be done. Game Play, I wish to sign up to be the first student at your Future Literacy Academy. Plato's Academy has needed a redo for two thousand years. And to be future literate, I agree with you, Game Play, that you must truly unpack all your assumptions and play in the abstract space of zeroth principles as much as possible. It's essential. And so what we should be asking ourselves about our biology and our biological future is: What are the zeros? Where are they? What's the lowest-hanging zero?"

Depression: "What I hear you pining for is a future without me. Do you imagine I won't exist in this highly programmable future?"

Blueprint: "I imagine that you will be made into a ... luxury good. Artists do all kinds of things for art. Salvador Dali used to have his wife rub his closed eyelids with a cotton ball on a long stick to create swirly, psychedelic visual impressions on the inside of his eyes. Nothing about a highly programmable biological future means that people won't have the choice to feel however they wish. This is one of the classic refrains of change, right? *But won't people think of the artists? What if we want to be sad? Some of the best works of art come from sadness.* Yes, yes. Everyone knows that it's a slightly more complicated question than, for example, whether we should get rid of smallpox or malaria or cancer. Even though the end is the same—reduced quality of life, pain, suffering—it is clear and evident that, though they too sometimes bring with them great art, life is better without them. It's not entirely clear to me how that's all that different than Depression—why wouldn't we get rid of it, too?—but maybe because something about the nature of sadness feels intrinsic to what it is to be alive, we want to keep it around, just in case, like a cabinet of emotional curiosities we refuse to throw away the key to, generation after generation."

Seeks Authority was standing under the door frame toward the sunroom. He had snuck back in.

Seeks Authority: "Personally, I'd throw away that key. I can't imagine anyone of any actual importance, strength, or ambition needing a crutch like *him*."

Self Critical: "I don't mind him at all. For as many things as he seems to make harder in life, he seems to make equal and opposite things easier. It feels zero-sum to me, and, depending on the mood or circumstance, the distribution of gain to loss favors gain sometimes. I agree with Blueprint's earlier claim, actually, which isn't something I thought I'd say. He's situationally useful.

Seeks Authority: "Sometimes, Self Critical, I watch you speak, and I watch your lips move, but I hear *his* voice." He pointed to Depression, who sat silently on the couch.

Blueprint: "This is exactly it, gentlemen. The nature of the debate about whether to keep the good or keep the bad or in what doses. Or in what circumstances. This is the very point. This is the very opportunity that the highly programmable future will provide us. Depending on individual wants or desires, you can choose such things. We can keep him or not. Much as you can choose to forgive or forget the past."

Model Builder: "Okay, but we can already choose our friends and sort of feel our way around control of our emotions. There are billions of dollars spent in the self-help industry every year promising just such a thing. And even if it only works five percent of the time, or even one percent, the point is *it works*. Every lifestyle insomniac knows that if they had total control of their environment, their stressors, and their worries in life, they could probably sleep perfectly if they dedicated themselves to it or treated it like rehab. They may never get there, but secretly, deep down, they know."

Blueprint: "Indeed, but it's *not* easy. Much is lost. We are all making such trade-offs constantly but crudely. Like people at the turn of the century who were harnessing only a fraction of nature's physical operating system—a shunt of electricity here, a piece of coal there—we in the biological programming world realize how little we can actually harness the control levers or potential of what is theoretically possible. For decades after the invention of electricity, streetlamps and home lights were still lit by oil or gasoline. It takes a long time for the theoretic inventions at the cutting edge to make their way into the home. All of the programmable biology we see in laboratories today, including all the counting and numbers and feedback loops and quantification available to the doctor or scientist, will be available in an easy-to-use package one day, which is like a personal body computer."

Farm Boy: "But how will I ever learn how to program my own body?"

Self Critical: "You won't."

Farm Boy: "Well, then what's the point?"

Self Critical: "That Blueprint thinks he already lives in the future. Have you noticed how little he speaks of the present? It's always either the past or the future. It's always about how something was or how something will be. It's all a grandiose bluster from someone afraid to be in the moment. It's very easy to value the future when you don't care about the present. It's the heart of motivation to flip temporal discounting on its head and somehow make the future *more* valuable than the present. But it's an illusion. The present is literally, always, forever and has always been the only thing that ever existed. The past equally doesn't exist the same way the future does. We only have right now. We only have right here. You don't need to worry, Farm Boy. The future will never arrive because even when it does, it will only be the present then, too."

Blueprint: "To more directly answer your worry, Farm Boy, can I ask: Do you have a smartphone? A cell phone?"

Farm Boy: "I have a flip phone with a few important numbers, yes. Here."

Blueprint: "I don't need to see it. I'm just curious if you have any idea whatsoever how to build one from scratch."

"A phone?"

"Yes."

"No."

"Most engineers today could not build a simple and functional *toaster*. It is actually extremely difficult to get all the pieces perfectly in place because bread is not just in simulation. It's in the real world, a physical object with variable sizes and shapes and textures and thicknesses and depending on all kinds of stuff, it can burn or not burn or be too thick or thin, and sometimes people put forks in them, etc., etc. You get the point. Just like how we can build robots to kick our butts in chess, but we can't build a robot that can walk down to Washington Square Park, sit down, and play a simple game with any set of arbitrary pieces. No, it needs its perfect world. Not the real world. Physical engineering requires interacting with the real world, which is a god-awful mess. It's relatively easy for software programmers to build things that only have to interact in the digital world. Software *likes* interacting with software. The pieces are mostly made to fit together. But when software tries to interact with the real world, things fall apart rapidly. At this point, each toaster leverages industrial-scale supply chains and specialized machinery impossible for any one person to replicate. I know it sounds simple at first. But the truth is we take for granted how much prior art and prior knowledge and tinkering and absolute mechanical genius and labor has gone into the world around us.

"And so, Farm Boy, my point is simply that you can use your phone, right? It's made to be readable by someone who cannot program or design microchips, right? You don't need to know how cell towers work or how your voice gets alchemically transduced into a signal and then uncompressed on the other end as it gets bounced around cell towers or satellites or whatnot. You just have to know a phone number and a name and what you want to do with the device. That's all. And so *of course* you're not going to need to know how to program your darn body. You'll get a few little buttons, like a thermostat, and you can tell it to turn to heat or cool and what your desired temperature is and everything else will do all the work. Just like every device ever. The point is not that we will all become programmers. The point is that the programming will be possible, and entire financial and technical ecosystems will sprout around the ability for an individual to pipe in their desires to their body and mind in a way that is unfathomable to us right now."

Model Builder looked like he finally understood. At least in part.

Model Builder: "And age will just be a variable?"

Blueprint: "Age will just be a variable, yes."

Self Critical: "Did you see the film *In Time*, Blueprint? Or did you, Zero?"

Blueprint: "No."

Self Critical: "The idea of it is that years of one's life can be traded, like a currency. It was mentioned earlier that with, what was it called, 'temporal discounting,' that one can make an exchange rate with biological futures, right? Well, in the movie, they just presume that not only can that happen within a body, but what works for one person can actually work for another person. Everyone is genetically modified to die at age twenty-six, and they have to earn more to keep going. And so you can *trade* years of your life. Minutes of your life is what most do. And people of course make markets out of it. There is a whole underground market for *minutes*. High-end poker games are played *for centuries*. People have a counter embedded in their arms. Society is entirely reconfigured around the idea, and the equivalent of bank robbers or Bonnie and Clyde steal *time* instead of money because obviously time becomes the most valuable resource, the most valuable commodity, in the history of the planet. It is, in essence, *the* primary nonfungible unit of concern in life."

Zero: "Fascinating."

Self Critical: "And can you guess what happens?"

Dark Humor: "Let me guess. Probably ... the rich live forever?"

Self Critical: "Yeah, pretty much. You sit down to a fancy dinner, and the menu is *in time.* A steak is like a thousand hours or something. A coffee is four minutes. You tip in weeks. So where do the haves get the time from, you ask? From the same place money always comes from. From the have-nots, of course. The display on your arm of the amount of time you have left becomes a kind of de facto visa and passport into certain exclusive parts of society. Junkies trade their winter coats for more time. So, let's say your plan works. Biology is programmable. The entire world is. How would you prevent age from becoming a commodity?"

Game Play: "*Prevent?* I'm confused. Is it not already one, Self Critical? Are we not here today because we heard Scribe is dying? We already live in such a world. Every one of us shaped our lives to deal with his, let's call it, his 'temporal misfortune.'"

Dark Humor: "Speaking of relative time, did you know the male lead in that movie is three years older than the woman who plays *his mother?* Hollywood is maybe more relativistic than Einstein. Or maybe that was a plot point. I forget. Anyway, more to the point, you can be a real asshole sometimes, Blueprint, can't you?"

Silence.

Dark Humor turned to me: "I like him, Scribe. Can we keep him? And maybe Zero, too?"

14: Out of the Blue

Q: Do we need Depression around?
Q: What is the alternative?

Dark Humor: "What's the end goal here, BP?"

And there it was. He got a nickname. Initials only. He was in. BP finally had some true converts in the room.

Blueprint responded fully, heartily, and without missing a beat: "The world is depressed and a death cult. But if you tell people this, it provokes a strong reaction from those who consider themselves 'not depressed.' They are each acting rationally according to what appear to be the realities of existence, that life is suffering and death is inevitable, two previously incontrovertible truths. Because if life is *not* inevitable suffering and death—if these 'incontrovertible' truths are anything but—then our existence can and must be rebuilt to align with these new realities. It is riddled with cognitive biases. Collectively, we temporally discount the future of our species. And it starts with the individual mind of the depressed person, which is often, and is perhaps *always*, its own worst enemy. I know this because I've been there."

Depression: "I knew it. I can see the age spots a mile away."

Blueprint: "My anti-aging and algorithmic solution toward diet and health and the quantification of every part of body and mind is *for me*. It is not for everyone, nor should it be. Some aren't cut out for it. Some don't need it. Some are too timid. Exploring the South Pole of biology isn't for everybody, but I've got that covered. But what about the amateurs? Well, some people don't even want to leave their house or see anything new ever. This isn't for them. But the people who at least want to see what the world has to offer? To learn the lessons that I learned? Those are who I talk to, meet with, and help. My project has a very clear, explicit purpose. It's not a vanity project. It's a survival project. I am fighting back against my social and natural programming. Perhaps you can tell that many of the tenets of my lifestyle resemble those of certain religions. Strictures about what to eat. When to eat. Habits to form and follow. Where to get one's advice. Where to get one's truth from. I know some of you here also grew up in a faith. I know everyone in this room has had hardship, but I doubt many of you have lost your story as deeply and profoundly as I once did. I doubt many of you have had the entirety of your worldview shattered, in slow motion, like a glacier receding from the Arctic before your eyes. I believe in the concept of the future of biological programming because I know it works because I've *been* programmed. By stories. By books. By the people around me who didn't just change my mind—they changed, as powerfully as any scientist could ever engineer, how my eyes saw the world. They changed how I smelled the flowers on my morning walks. They changed what I saw in the cloud formations. They changed how I saw *people.* We are not simply programmable in the limit or with our tools—our minds are programmable by our very nature. It is our essence and our fate. Nature has given us the firmware, and language does the rest.

"The frameshift that was required to undo my social, ethical, aesthetic, and moral programming meant that absolutely everything was up for grabs once I saw the other side. Perhaps only those who have left a religion understand. Personally, I've never met anyone else who gets me the way that someone else who has left a religion does. And it can be anyone. Truly. They're all the same wooly blankets. Strangely, almost paradoxically, I had never seen the world more clearly than I did after I became convinced that religion not only wasn't for me but that eons of my growth and personal life had been stolen away from me. Harvested. Because once I saw what was on the other side, it was horrifying. It was meaningless. It was physics and the big bang and entropy and the inevitable *fact* of the heat death of the universe. *Fact.* You know the feeling when you wake up from a fall in a dream? The feeling that your stomach has dropped out from under you and your viscera are being stretched thin like baker's dough? It was like that but constant. Every second of every day. There's a musical illusion where it sounds like a pitch is always rising called the Shephard tone. It can drive someone mad. There's a perceived story when you listen to it because it sounds like the tones are getting higher and higher *toward something*. But they don't. They aren't. It's an endless loop of sound that goes toward no destination created by adding octaves to an original note. Which has no end. And which the human mind *cannot* perceive as it actually is. The sound is a sound from somewhere else, a sound like it is climbing higher and higher toward some infinitely high sound no human has ever heard before. *But it never gets there*. And the illusion can go infinitely up or infinitely down depending on which note you start at. Now imagine the feeling of one's stomach dropping just like that, in a loop, as if it's going toward something, as if it will one day stop, but it never does. It just keeps dropping. And dropping. And dropping. As if one is constantly waking up from a dream in an infinite loop.

"The only rational response to this is to cling desperately to someone like Depression here. He is the friend who will tell you the truth. He is the only one who will tell you that there really is nothing out there. That we really are alone. That the infinite tone is just a trick. That the stories your brain tells itself are lies. Of course, he would occasionally go too far and wouldn't leave the room when asked, but that's the price we all pay sometimes for ground-truth honesty in those moments of cathartic, divisive darkness.

"But my depression wouldn't leave. It aged me. It deflated me. I was accelerating toward the grave, and I just kept pulling it closer and closer. I couldn't just leave him on a mountain like it seemed you guys all could. We were attached at the hip. And so, after years of this, I got angry. I got fed up. And the first thing I wanted to do was reverse the aging. I was of course told it couldn't be done by many of the leading experts and scientists. It could theoretically be done, of course, but we didn't seem to know enough about the human body to do it predictably."

Zero, shaking his head: "Figures they would say that."

Blueprint: "But there's a funny skill and strength you get when your entire worldview is revealed to you one day as a sham. This will sound strange but ... suddenly, everything seems possible. And you can really see assumptions for what they really are. You become guarded to anybody who says the world is only one way and that *it has to be that way and there is no alternative.* But what if there was? Once you have the painful experience of coming to the conclusion on your own that there is more out there and that authority on truth comes in both degrees and kinds, you really start to live. You really start to, as you might like, Game Play, you really start to see that there are more infinite games out there than you first realized.

Game Play: "I feel like you were already always one of us, BP. You are saying things many of us resonate with. And I thank you for your honesty. Zero, you too seem to make sense in this room. Do we all agree?"

Seeks Authority: "Agree."

Game Play: "Ditto."

Farm Boy: "Right, true."

Dark Humor: "Even I'll admit it. You both fit. The room already wouldn't seem the same without you. Good find, Scribe. Good find, Game Play."

Game Play: "Zero here is an author, too. A small book called *Zeroism*. He could help you with the book, Scribe."

"Noted," I said. I gave Zero a little nod, a universal *Let's talk later* signal.

Depression, sourly: "I could take us or leave us. I do, in fact, have to go. I'm sorry I didn't get one-on-one time with everyone. Please, send my regards to all your missuses, for those lucky enough to corral one. Seems I've been replaced anyway. My only benefit to the group was saying the surprising thing nobody else would dare to. Dark and Humor and Zero seem to do just fine at that."

Model Builder: "This isn't that, friend."

Depression: "It sure seems it."

Blueprint: "Take my number. My email. Write me. There's some stuff we can try. Low-hanging fruit."

Depression: "You don't seem to understand that not everyone *wants* to be changed, do you? Some people like the path they're on. Anyone want to come with me? I'm going to a movie. Maybe a bar after. Steak. Potatoes. Gravy. Seventeen or so whiskeys until sunrise. That's my night. I can't wait. Who's in?"

Seeks Authority: "I think, actually, I'm supposed to be meeting someone at that same theater."

Depression: "I don't recall saying where I'm going. But sure, join, old pal."

Self Critical: "I'd love to see a movie with you guys. I'm in."

Cognitive Bias: "Well if everyone's leaving, I will too."

Classic CB. He always did overfit to recency.

Model Builder seemed offended: "Am I missing something, gentlemen? This is Scribe's going-away party. His *forever* going-away party."

Depression was already walking out the door. Without turning his back to respond, he made his punctuation mark for the evening: "Most of the world isn't here attending either. I don't think we'll be missed. Besides, I have hope you'll get through whatever it is you're going through, Scribe."

And with that, only a few remained in the room: Me, Model Builder, Game Play, Zero, Blueprint, Relentless, and Dark Humor.

Dark Humor: "And then there were six. Seven. Forgot about you, Zero."

Zero: "It happens. I like hiding in plain sight."

"Like Agatha Christie," I said. "*And Then There Were Six.* But no murder necessary here."

Dark Humor: "Glad *you* said it. Because I was *this* close to finishing the job myself."

15: What Now?

Seriously, though...
Q: What now?

All the remaining people had gathered in the room. Model Builder: "What next, Scribe?"

I responded, "Perhaps you can all tell me. Anyone have any pebbles?"

Nobody. On Mt. K, our group had decided on the concept of pebbles as a kind of social amelioration and friction defusal tactic. Rather than let a pebble sit in someone's shoe—metaphorically, of course—it is best to talk it out before it becomes a problem. We all agreed, as we would on the mountain itself, that if someone had a pebble in their shoe, we would all stop and wait for them to move on. And there could be no begrudging the pause, no matter how small the pebble.

It was an incredibly useful strategy for the horribly demanding mental conditions on the mountain. It worked so well we kept it in real life.

"Great," I said.

No immediate pebbles was a good sign. The most important part about asking if a group had any pebbles was to recognize any power imbalances and smooth them out into pearls. Sometimes people just sat silently on their pebble despite any and all entreaties not to, and there were two classic ways to draw anyone out of their silence: one, to announce your own tiny pebble, to get the pebbles rolling, so to speak; next, a prolonged, awkward silence. There was no better way than silence to get people to speak. Often, silence sits like an anxious void until human language comes along and fills it. One can only imagine how anxious the first few hundred thousand years of Ice Age man must have been. And so I sat. Silent.

Model Builder: "Well, I do have one. Blueprint, I've been considering your argumentative move to scale up the sensing, feedback, and algorithms that run a body to run the world. In a way, it's a novel and modern twist on the Gaia hypothesis, right? I like it. Did you know the guy who invented the theory was a chemist who worked at NASA? Few people do. It's real science. Not the hippy mumbo jumbo it became. In that theory, organic and inorganic life work together to form a sort of control system that regulates the conditions for all of life on Earth. It's a beautiful, heavily scientific idea. I ultimately think the science side is correct. You seem to be arguing something similar, Blueprint, ... that we can treat the planet in all its complexity as just a specialized case of biology, as a huge single organism with explicit organs that work together to keep the biological needs in a kind of entropic harmony. So what you're *really* doing with Blueprint is coming up with dedicated algorithms for understanding highly complex biological systems and, once the details are worked out for the body, we can expand things to tackle the entire planet? It makes sense. Many of the tools required to navigate and do closed-loop feedback control *should* scale. Not the exact details, of course, just the larger-scale concepts. The entire suite of chemical and physical sensors fused with the fanciest AI and robotics can be made to tackle the *longevity of Earth.* I get it. I see through you. That's what this is really about, isn't it? Ultimately, we need to keep Earth's temperature in check the same way a huge amount of our internal systems keeps our mammalian temperatures in check. Just like how sometimes we have a fever, it seems that right now, in the earliest part of the twentieth century, the Earth has a fever too.

"But I admit that I'm stuck on the demotion of the conscious mind part of your theory, Blueprint. Why is that necessary? I know, I know, I'm sorry to bring it back up again because I see that it's clearly something not everybody agrees on. And I do agree that humanity has led itself into some dark, existential corners. We have put our entire species and much of our lives at stake for the sake of a few tribal disputes multiple times in the last century alone. The very first century that we had doomsday devices we nearly used them multiple times. We were a few button pushes away from global annihilation. Clearly, we don't value our future selves. Clearly, we are extracting everything we can out of the oceans and land and letting it back into our lungs and atmosphere. Clearly, people just sort of volunteer for dystopia as long as they get social media and sugar and don't get lost anymore. But what I don't quite buy is the idea that Gaia is depressed right now. We do seem to be upward trending in terms of global awareness, global empathy. So why then the idea that we must *demote* a version of the conscious mind and not *promote* one? The way I have heard you speak today, it seems like I hear or imagine two paths. One demotes the conscious mind. One uplevels it with AI, technology, sensors, sleep, diet, etc. So which is it? I can't quite tell. Sorry if that's too big a pebble, Scribe. I just haven't been able to fully wrap my mind around the single path forward."

"No problem at all, Model Builder," I said. "Blueprint? Any response?"

Dark Humor: "Can I ask a favor? This isn't because I have nothing to respond with or wish to burden anyone. But sometimes it can be very helpful to hear other people summarize what they've heard so far. Could anyone else answer Model Builder's question? BP will just say the same thing again, and if we don't get it by now, we're not magically going to just by hearing it again. Anyone?"

Zero: "I'd actually like to try, if I may. A great playwright, Tom Stoppard, once said that laughter is the sound of comprehension. My goal will be to get you to laugh at the end. I need to start with a digression, though. There's this idea in both comedy and video games called negative transfer. The idea is that a rapid switching of one's frame, in the comedy case, or control scheme, in the video game case, can be both funny and frustrating. As a simple example, think about playing a Nintendo game and you've learned since the beginning of time that the left little button on the D-pad moves your character left and the 'A' button makes him jump. And then imagine some sort of spell in the game and suddenly all the controls are reversed. That's called a negative transfer. You've learned something, and then suddenly you don't just have to unlearn it, *you actually start out at a disadvantage because you've learned the opposite way*. Hence, the 'negative' part in negative transfer. The analog in comedy is the idea that throughout the sketch you've defined the rules of the tiny universe the sketch or joke is taking place in, and then, suddenly, everything you know is used against you.

"One of the better jokes that showcases this is about a captain and he's out on the water and there's another ship up ahead. It's nighttime, and they can only see each other's lights. And so the captain confidently gets on the radio—it's a big US Navy vessel, after all, top of the fleet—and says, 'This is the captain of the USS *Whatever*. Change course to port immediately.' The response comes in over the radio: 'Hello, captain of the USS *Whatever*, I request instead that *you* change course immediately.' To which the captain doubles down back to the oncoming ship and says, 'This is the captain of the USS *Whatever*, the flagship of the US Navy. We have a whole carrier battalion behind us. Suggest you change course to port immediately.' Seconds later the response comes back: 'Hello, captain of the USS *Whatever*, flagship of the US Navy, this is a lighthouse.'

"See, you start the joke knowing too much. You think it's another boat and that there are rules of the sea. The captain undergoes a kind of negative transfer as he has to learn that 'pressing left' on the D-pad—in the analogy, pressing left here is signaling over the radio what *usually* and *used to* work and telling a boat that it is the US Navy, which has *always* worked for him in the past—doesn't work anymore. His control scheme has changed. This has the added benefit of being what's called a diegetic, which means 'within the narrative.' The captain is learning the same lesson that the listener of the joke is learning as they learn it. A diegetic is, oh, what's a good example ... think of a movie soundtrack. Real life doesn't have a soundtrack, right? Is it kind of weird then that movies do? Some movies solve this by introducing diegetic—again, within the narrative—music. So when the characters themselves can hear the music, we do too. And so occasionally in movies you'll have a character push play on their cassette tape or smartphone or streaming service or whatever in the car, and it is both the soundtrack to the movie and what the character is listening to, which brings you, the viewer, together with the character.

"And so, Dark Humor, I can hear you all saying, 'What's this all got to do with the conscious mind?' Well, I think one aspect of the beauty of Blueprint's idea is that it's fundamentally, if you think about it, a negative transfer. It's flipping the way the world is supposed to work on its head because the very existence and power of the conscious mind is that you are supposed to trust it. The conscious mind exists so that you trust it. It evolved so that you both are it and *have* to trust it in a sense. It creates your

228

entire reality. It is the ultimate worldview. It is the only omniscient deity for which we have actual evidence. And we each get one. We each get our own, personal deity defining how the world should be perceived, what colors it has, what's important, what's not, etc. And so the important thing to realize is that we will all start at a disadvantage if we follow Blueprint's theory to its logical conclusion because we must use the default mind that we've all come to know and love against itself. The control pad is suddenly different again. The way reality is constructed becomes different. Evening Dark Humor is used to considering himself a full entity and conscious creature with willpower and consciousness and all the stuff that makes us *us* and him *him*. But now left makes you go right. A 'go' signal from the hypothalamus for hunger is a 'stop' signal. Left is right. Up is down. It's Dr. Seussean. But the most important part, as I see it, is that this is also a diegetic approach because—this is the key point—our planet is not conscious. Our species is not conscious. There is no one thing that it is like to be conscious.

"So in that sense, Model Builder, with all due respect, it's actually extremely *different* from the Gaia theory, which posits a sort of coevolved sentience between organic and inorganic life. In actual fact, it's a dumb rock with a bunch of individuals clinging desperately to a blip to existence and trying their hardest through all kinds of chicanery to pass along their silly little attempts to stay alive. That's it. There is no actual being up there. There is no creature in the planet's core caring about how hot the planet gets. And so when you add up all of the parts you realize that what Blueprint is saying is not to demote the conscious mind in order to lose it in itself but, instead, to *mirror* what we are trying to save. It's diegetic. It's the equivalent of having a movie playing a soundtrack and then suddenly, in one scene, in a car, they push pause, and the music stops, and we, the audience, realize that the character has been listening to what we've been hearing all along too. It's that moment. So, if I had to guess, Model Builder, I'd say that that is your confusion. It's not a demotion. It's a promotion to a kind of accuracy otherwise unachievable.

"And Blueprint here, to me, just sounds like he's been going on a WHO and UNICEF mission in his body to clean up the rivers, bring back the fresh-water dolphins, so to speak, de-acidify the oceans, and put things back into order. The circulatory system is obviously our planet's waterways. Our organs are biodiversity. The forests, its lungs. You can map the metaphor onto however you wish, but like our planet's waterways, which are polluted and clogged, and our lungs are burning, and yet, still we con-sume. Yet still we eat the midnight oil snack. That's what the power of this approach is. To prove that through algorithms alone, without letting the pesky mind get in the way and not because it's necessarily harmful but simply because there *should be a way without it.*

"Humanity is in the process of giving birth to a new form of intelligence more capable of certain tasks than we will ever be. We are merely its shepherd. And according to the Gaia idea, this is totally normal. Just as it took billions of years for the algae to excrete their waste product, oxygen, into the atmosphere to allow complex life to form, we have been spending the last tens of thousands of years creating the conditions for inorganic, artificial life, in the form of silicon or diamond or whatever fancy information-processing device future AI will use, to take over again. Think about a dragonfly or a plant, which sees the world at very different timescales than we do. To the future AIs that we can align with and that will run and keep in check the full complexities of our biosphere, we will appear to move at the same speed as we view plants. They can respond to events thousands, maybe millions, of times faster than we could ever hope to. The pace of our thinking is glacial relative to what they will achieve. And if I hear Blueprint right, I think what he's saying is: 'The conscious mind lives at the wrong timescale to solve humanity's biggest problems.' And it's true. It does. We have no hope. Our only chance is creating and training an intelligence so profoundly strong it can cancel out our mistakes and bring us into a new era of prosperity. We won't be the supreme form of intelligence anymore, but that's okay. Why do we need to be? Ego? Shame? We'll get over it. The world will be so unimaginably different it's almost not worth contemplating with our puny, Paleolithic minds how we will change. Think about the difference between how to tell heart health through human means alone—stick two fingers on some blood vessels and count to sixty—versus what we can do in a hospital with angiograms, contrast dyes, EKGs, etc. *Those tools are tools of certain timescales*. We just need a suite of AI-powered tools to take the heartbeat of the planet, so to speak, to understand the complexity of its interactions with tools of timescale, and to keep this whole thing running.

Blueprint stood, smiled, and offered his hand to Zero.

Blueprint: "So you *were* listening, Zero. May I call you *friend*? That was one succinct and beautiful summary. Thank you. And I agree entirely with your points. Thank you. That actually helps me realize a few things I have wondered about myself."

I figured now, if ever, was the time. I said, "Okay, now that those who wish to be here are still here, I have one last agenda item."

Dark Humor: "Mini golf? Please say mini golf."

"Alas."

Dark Humor: "*Hrmph.*"

Finally, I could reveal my plan. Not *The Plan*, just yet. But my plan is to get to The Plan.

I said, "There are many scales and levels in which society is programmed. As you said earlier, Blueprint, sometimes this is in the unwritten social rules of organizations or tribes. Other times, like with various nation-state constitutions or religious creeds, they are explicitly written down. That's what I want us to do with the time we have left today. I want us to work together and write down a capital-P Plan for Humanity using all of these ideas. I have no children. Unlike many of you here, I want my legacy to be the work you all will have to shepherd into reality together. I am content with my ambition and accomplishments in life. I live peacefully and vicariously through the four beautiful children my closest friends here today have. They are our legacy. They are who we owe everything to. The future does exist because it will, and I ask that we do the opposite of temporal discounting. I want *temporal inflation*. I want us to embrace the view that, for the next few hours until I keel over in exhaustion, we are Shackleton's crew on the *Endurance*. It's a year in. We've been through hell. But we persist. We keep going. Everything we thought we knew about preferences or discipline is out the window. They ate seal stew for years. On Elephant Island, they slept in frozen, wet sleeping bags and every morning carried buckets of water from their makeshift tent, which was just an upturned boat with some wind protection. And yet still, every single morning, without fail, no matter what, no matter how few calories they had or how much they ached or wanted to give up, they climbed to the highest point of the mountain, looking and hoping for rescue. That is the mindset I want us to embrace. We write until I die. That's my final wish. Are you in? Are you *all in*? I am going to transcribe today and its conversations, like Plato did with Socrates. And at the end, I will add what this has all been working toward: The Plan."

And at that moment, I knew what I would become on my death.

Ashes to ashes?

Dust to dust?

No.

Ink to ink.

Paper to paper.

About the Author

Zero was the first individual *H. sapiens* to surpass five hundred years of age. He died in 2478, hit by Earth's last bus in operation, only weeks before becoming Homo Deus. During his life, Zero fathered millions of biological and digital offspring who now live in the far reaches of the solar system and beyond. Best known for inventing Zeroism and the resurrection technology *undie*, Zero famously raised his detractors from the dead so he could tell them that he had outlived them.

Zero's ancestor, Bryan Johnson, was born in twentieth-century USA. Johnson left his religious upbringing and built the payments company Braintree Venmo, which sold to PayPal for eight hundred million dollars in 2013. He subsequently became a pioneering entrepreneur and investor in the fields of synthetic biology, nanotechnology, brain interfaces, and longevity. Johnson became the most biologically measured person in history through his Project Blueprint and created the global movement DON'T DIE that sowed the seeds for human, planetary, and AI alignment.

Printed in Great Britain
by Amazon